The water was up to our necks now. With each ebb and flow of the tide we had to jump and lift Dad above the rising swell. Bones floated all around us, making eerie clicking noises as they bumped into each other.

I knew our time was running out.

The Buzzard's Treasure

by Cindy Savage

To Brian and Lisa

cover illustration by Richard Kriegler

Published by Willowisp Press
801 94th Avenue North, St. Petersburg, Florida 33702

Printed in the United States of America

2 4 6 8 10 9 7 5 3 1

ISBN 0-87406-673-5

CONTENTS

CHAPTER 1
On Board the Buzzard's Bounty

"THREE centuries! Just imagine, Brian," my sister Lisa exclaimed as we sailed into Victoria harbor. "The Buzzard's treasure has stayed hidden on tiny Mahé Island for almost three hundred years!"

"If anyone can find it, Dad can," I told her as I scanned the lights reflecting on the water in the bay. "I just hope it takes him longer this time."

"Why do you say that?" Lisa asked as she turned her back on the lights and peered into my face. "You know that our father is the best treasure hunter on the high seas. You can't be wishing him bad luck on his dream treasure hunt. I mean, all of the other hunts—digging up the frozen ship in Alaska and diving for the pearls from the *Charming Mary* off the coast of the Bahamas, even uncovering that temple in Peru—they all led up to this one, the Buzzard's treasure."

7

I leaned back and took a deep breath of the salty ocean air. Overhead the sky was perfectly clear above Mahé Island, the largest island in the Seychelles chain, smack in the middle of the Indian Ocean off the coast of Africa.

"I know," I said, sighing. "Don't you think I practically have the Buzzard's legend memorized by now? Almost every day since I was a little kid I've heard all about the twelve clues and the coded parchment that the dreaded French pirate, Olivier le Vasseur, whose name means *buzzard* in French, left behind before he was hanged. Sometimes I feel like a dead pirate is running my life!"

"I thought you liked treasure hunting," Lisa said.

"I do," I said quickly. "I just wish sometimes that we could be like other kids. You know—stay in one place for more than a minute, go to a regular school, play on a sports team, have lots of friends. I mean, you're 13 and I'm 15—how many other kids our age do you know who live on a ship ten months out of the year?"

"None," Lisa admitted. "But I know plenty who would be glad to quit school and do what we do. *Some* people think that sailing around the world in search of buried treasure is an adventure! Most kids have told me that they'd love to have the famous Stephen Chaffier as their dad."

"Until they got to know him," I muttered under my breath. *Until they found out that he cares more for his doubloons and pieces of eight and treasure maps and secret codes than he does for his own family,* I thought.

"Pardon me?" Lisa asked, leaning close.

I decided to change the subject. "At least Mahé seems like an interesting place to explore," I said.

Lisa shook her head. As usual, she probably knew what I was thinking. Most other guys usually don't get along with their sisters, but I don't have much choice. Most of the time she's the only one around, and it gets pretty boring in the middle of the ocean without someone to talk to. Dad's always busy charting courses and dredging up lost artifacts. Mom's always writing books about our trips, so Lisa and I end up entertaining each other. The only trouble with being close is that I can't hide my feelings from her.

"You don't fool me, Brian Chaffier," Lisa declared. "You're as excited about staying on Mahé as I am. Tomorrow we're going to start school—a real school—and we're going to live in a house on shore. I've been reading about Mahé and there are jungles, beaches, and mountains to hike around on. And Dad says he's going to take it easy while he searches for the Buzzard's treasure."

"I hope you're right," I said. "I guess we'll find out soon enough. Only one more night on the ship and then tomorrow we start our new life as landlubbers."

"Hey, Brian, Lisa!" Dad called from the helm. "Lend a hand, you two. We're about to drop anchor."

Lisa hurried to her place by the anchor windlass and waited for Dad's signal. I ran to the bow and looked over.

"I've brought the bow into the wind," Dad called.

"I've released the brake on the winch and the anchor's ready to run," Lisa called.

I watched the anchor drop and followed the line of the chain as it dropped into the clear water. "She's on the bottom," I called. "You can back her down."

Lisa let out additional anchor chain as Dad pulled the ship tight against the anchor.

"The scope looks good," I said as I took note of the angle of the chain. There was just enough to allow our ship, the *Buzzard's Bounty*, to swing slightly with the wind. "The anchor's set!"

"I'm shutting her down," Dad said. "Good job, kids."

Joe, our cook, poked his head out of the

galley just as we had secured the ship for the night. "How about supper on the deck tonight, Captain?"

Dad looked up at the canopy of stars just beginning to appear in the twilight sky and smiled. "Good plan. We can all enjoy the water one last night before we go ashore."

"I'll help bring up the grub," Lisa offered. "Where's Mom?"

"The last time I saw her she was hunched over her computer, trying to finish off the last chapter of the *Charming Mary* story," Joe said.

"I'll go let her know that supper's ready," Dad said.

I waited on deck with the other members of the crew—four besides Joe, who had sailed with us, on and off, for the past several years. There was Hawk, the first mate, Luke, Chester, and William. Manuel was the only new crew member. He signed on in Peru after we came out of the jungle. Looking at them in the dark, they almost looked like real pirates. Their clothes were dirty, they hadn't shaved for a while, and their hair was either shaved off or long and scraggly—except for Chester, who wore his back in a ponytail.

I shook my head. But of course they weren't pirates. Hawk has a Ph.D. in marine biology. Chester is a diver and a historian and worked for the National Maritime museum. Luke is the ship's engineer. William is an archeologist, and Manuel is a cartographer—that's a person who draws and interprets maps. We needed him to help decipher the old maps of Mahé Island. When we aren't hunting treasure, everybody doubles as deckhands.

"Hey! Everyone ready for the grub?" Joe called as he crossed the deck balancing a couple of trays of food. Lisa came right behind him carrying three jugs of juice. She had a tablecloth draped over her shoulder and a stack of plastic glasses gripped under her chin.

Hawk jumped up to assist her. "Need some help, little lady?" he asked in a gravelly voice.

"Thanks," Lisa said, releasing the glasses and one of the jugs.

"Look alive, maties," Hawk announced. "The captain's on deck."

Chester and Luke laid the tablecloth on the deck. William set the plates and silverware around in a circle while Manuel unloaded Joe's trays.

"Beautiful night, gentlemen," Mom said, greeting the crew. "Hi kids," she added to Lisa and me. "I'll bet you're getting impatient to be on land again."

"I like it at sea, Mom," Lisa said.

"But it will be nice to stay in one place for a while," Dad said, echoing my thoughts. "Everyone deserves a break after our jungle trek. We'll just take the Buzzard's treasure slowly and easily. After all, the treasure has been buried for three hundred years—I doubt that a few more weeks will make a difference."

"Everyone eat the stew while it's still hot," Joe added with a laugh. "If you get to talking about the Buzzard, the stew will be as cold as he is and twice as dead!"

Dad laughed. "Better dish up, everyone. Before Joe throws us all overboard."

"Or makes us walk the plank," Chester joked.

After supper, Dad got out his guitar and Mom snuggled over next to him. Seeing them sitting together on the deck, no one would guess that Stephen Chaffier is one of the most famous treasure hunters in the world, and Margeaux Chaffier is a well-known author with seven published adventure books. They looked just like anyone else's parents.

Our last name is French—pronounced Shaw-fee-ay. Dad's parents came from France, and Dad speaks French fluently. He says it really helps when he's trying to read old maps, like the ones the Buzzard left.

Beneath me, I felt the gentle roll of the ship's deck as I listened to my father pluck out a sea ballad on his guitar.

"Do you think we'll really find the Buzzard's treasure?" Lisa whispered next to me. "People have been searching for years and no one has had any luck. Maybe the Buzzard played a giant joke on us all."

"Maybe," I said, raising my head and looking out across the harbor. "I guess I really don't care whether we find it or not. I'm just ready to settle down."

"Brian, what do you think it will be like?" Lisa asked.

"What?" I said.

"Going to a real school for the first time. Aren't you a little nervous?" she asked. "We start tomorrow."

"I think it will be fun," I said. "We'll get to meet a lot of kids and maybe I'll join a sports team. *If* we stay long enough . . . "

"Dad promised we'd be here awhile," Lisa reminded me quietly.

"I know," I said, sighing. "Dad says that finding the Buzzard's treasure will be his last hurrah and then he'll quit. But you know Dad. He has treasure hunting in his blood. He's too young to quit."

"Quit?" Dad boomed across the circle. "Who said anything about quitting? We've just begun this adventure!"

Oh, no! Here comes the story again, I thought.

"Reginald Herbert Cruise-Wilkins didn't quit, and neither will I," Dad declared.

"Cruise-Wilkins died before he found the treasure," I said.

"Well, I don't intend to do that," Dad said with a laugh. "Besides, our old buddy Reginald did most of the work for us. All we have to do is pick up where he left off."

"You never did tell me the story of the Buzzard," Manuel, the newest crew member, said. "I want to hear it while we're sitting in the very same harbor that the Buzzard sailed into so many years ago. Maybe I should know more about the old pirate before I try to figure out his island."

I rolled my eyes and looked at Lisa. We could both tell the story of the Buzzard backward and forward with our eyes closed.

"I don't know if you really want to hear it, Manuel," Hawk warned playfully, his eyes gleaming. "I hope you're not scared of ghosts."

"Not me," Manuel said. "We're all going to be ghosts sooner or later."

Dad strummed his guitar and then picked out a few notes of a haunting melody. The crew members were silent as he began to speak. Manuel leaned forward.

"Olivier le Vasseur was born in France in 1690. He was only a little older than Brian, here, when King Louis XV gave him permission to become a privateer. For years he sailed the sea, attacking the ships of France's enemies and sharing his captured treasure with his king."

"But he got greedy," Lisa added.

"Greedy, yes," Dad agreed, strumming his guitar with one quick motion. "He broke his side of the bargain and became a pirate. He began to seize vessels from all countries, including France. King Louis was furious. In 1720 he offered a large reward for the Buzzard's capture. But it wasn't until 1730 that the notorious pirate was caught and sentenced to death by hanging."

I shivered in spite of the warm air and unconsciously rubbed my throat. I looked up to see Hawk's dark eyes trained on me and for a second I felt like prey. But that was silly—I'd known Hawk for years and he was our friend and a good crew member. I took my hand down and turned back to Dad.

"But the Buzzard had a sense of humor even in the face of death," Dad continued. "As he mounted the scaffold to the waiting noose, he threw a roll of parchment to the crowd below. With a loud, fiendish laugh, he shouted, 'Find my treasure, to him who can understand!'"

"And on the parchment were twelve lines of coded writing," I added, caught up once again in the story that I had grown up with. "And there were some drawings and numbers leading to his treasure hidden somewhere on an island in the Indian Ocean. But no one could figure them out. Everyone thought the secret of the treasure died with the Buzzard."

Dad plucked the strings on his guitar to show the passing of years. "In 1756, the Seychelles Islands were settled by a group of French people, including the Savy family. They began to farm the land on the island of Mahé. But it wasn't until 1920 that one of their descendants, Mrs. Charles Savy, noticed a strangely shaped rock sticking out of the ocean at low tide."

Lisa leaned forward to interrupt. "When she looked at the rock closely, she saw carved pictures of animals and a large eye on one side. Mrs. Savy had her workers dig beneath the rock and they found—"

"Hey, who's telling this story?" Dad asked, chuckling.

Lisa grinned. "You are."

"Well, then," he said, lowering his voice, "the workers made a grisly discovery. They found two coffins with human bones. Gold

17

pieces and pirate earrings lay beneath each grinning skull and each bony hand held a cutlass."

"Lots of pirates used Seychelles as a hiding place," Manuel said. "It could have been any of them."

"Yes, but Mrs. Savy found an old map in a trunk in her attic, drawn in Portugal in 1729. On it, scrawled in ink, were the words, 'owner of land . . . the Buzzard.' She also tracked down a copy of his roll of parchment, but no matter how hard she tried, she couldn't decode the twelve lines of writing," Dad said. "Can you imagine, knowing that you lived on land that held untold riches, but not being able to solve the puzzle?"

"That's probably why she talked to Cruise-Wilkins about it," Mom reasoned. "She was probably so frustrated that by the time Cruise-Wilkins came to Mahé to recover from an illness she'd have talked to anyone."

Dad nodded and continued. "Cruise-Wilkins was fascinated by the story of the Buzzard's treasure. He already had a bit of the adventurer in him, since he was a big-game hunter in East Africa. He spent the next five months trying to unravel the mysterious words and diagrams on the parchment. Bit by bit he figured out the first of the twelve lines. The first clue was 'a woman, water-logged, dig at her feet.'

"He found the first clue, a large, flat rock with markings like a compass point," Dad continued. "He dug hole after hole, only to find nothing. Then one day he uncovered a stone statue of a woman. As he watched, sea water seeped slowly through the sand to puddle around the statue."

"A woman, water-logged," Hawk growled softly. "He couldn't give up after that."

"I suppose not," Manuel admitted. "It sure intrigues me."

"Twenty-eight years," Dad said with a sigh. "He found eleven out of twelve clues. He was sure that he had finally figured out the last line of writing, but he died, ill and penniless, before he could find the treasure. And he took his knowledge of the last clue to his grave with him."

"Perhaps the treasure wasn't meant to be found," Chester said, his voice low. "A lot of people have died trying to find it since Cruise-Wilkins. What if there's a curse? Maybe you'll die, too."

I stared at Chester. He was deadly serious. It almost sounded as if he were threatening Dad.

"Curses don't bother me," Dad said lightly. "The *Charming Mary* was supposedly guarded by a sea monster, but it turned out to be a giant squid. The Inca temple was supposedly protected by booby traps, but they had all rotted away by the time we found it.

"But there was a rumor . . . " Dad continued, leaning forward and lowering his voice. He looked me straight in the eye. "Some people think that after the Buzzard was hanged in France, his ghost returned to Mahé to protect his stash. The island people have reported hearing the jingle of chains late at night, along with the clash of cutlasses. They say that at midnight, at Deadman's Cove, if you listen very carefully, you can hear the wind carrying the sound of rollicking pirate's tunes, sung to the beat of a shovel digging in the sand."

CHAPTER 2
New Friends

"**Y**OU look awful!" Lisa told me the next morning as we walked up the gravel pathway to Jean Francois Hodoul school. It didn't take us long to move our stuff from the boat into the furnished house we'd rented.

"Thanks a heap!" I snarled. "I didn't get much sleep last night."

"Worried about starting tenth grade? I'm sure you'll do fine, Brian. Mom said we're probably ahead of the students here because we've done so much studying on our own."

"I'm not worried at all about school. I told you, I'm looking forward to going. I just kept hearing noises, that's all."

"What kind of noises?" Lisa asked. "The ship always creaks and groans a lot when it's at anchor."

I ran my hand through my hair. "Not those kinds of noises. I heard footsteps and somebody dragging something. And people were talking in low voices just outside my cabin."

"Who was talking? Some of the crew members?"

"That's just it. I don't know. I didn't recognize the voices. I wonder if someone came on the ship after we went to bed. I thought I heard chains or something metallic clang against the side of the ship."

Lisa shook her head. "You're probably just imagining things. Dad told us all those stories about the Buzzard's ghost and you heard chains and footsteps. Are you sure you weren't dreaming about pirates?"

"I don't think I was," I replied. "I don't think I got enough sleep last night to have any dreams."

"Why didn't you go check it out?"

I didn't want to tell her that I had been just a little scared. Maybe it had been hearing the ghost stories, I don't know, but the footsteps, the voices—I guess I didn't really want to know. I mean, what if it were just a couple of the guys from the crew? They would have laughed themselves silly if I had sneaked up on them.

"Uhh, I guess I was too tired," I said, looking away so that she wouldn't see that I was lying. I didn't want my sister to know that I had been spooked the night before.

When we went into the school office we saw a woman sitting behind a desk. "Hello," she said. "You must be Brian and Lisa Chaffier. We've been expecting you. Your parents have already sent the papers and documents we need."

I smiled and stepped up to the desk. "Here are our records from the correspondence school we've been attending," I said, handing her a manila envelope full of papers. "Lisa is supposed to be in the eighth grade and I'm supposed to be in tenth."

"I'm sure we'll find the right classrooms for you. I'm Mrs. Hulet, the school secretary," she told us. "If you'll follow me, I'll introduce you to your new teachers."

Mrs. Hulet spoke with an English accent like some the people on the island, but it was pretty easy to understand her. Seychelles had been a British territory for a time.

She showed us around the school, pointing out different things and answering our questions. The classrooms were in a circle around a courtyard filled with flowers and gardens.

"Do you have any sports teams?" I asked. I looked around, but didn't see a gymnasium.

"The children play football, or what you may know as soccer—it's the national game of the Seychelles. We also have a rowing team, cross-country track team, and goggling team," Mrs. Hulet said.

"Goggling?" I asked.

"Swimming under water," she explained.

"Where's the pool?"

Mrs. Hulet laughed. "We swim in the ocean. We rope off lanes in the lagoon and race out there."

"Cool. I can't wait," I said, smiling.

* * * * *

By the end of the day, Lisa and I had attended six classes and I really liked it. It was fun meeting all of the kids and moving from class to class. I liked the science room best. The rows of specimens on the wall reminded me of Hawk's quarters on the ship. He was always collecting something and wanted to own his own research company one day.

Mom had been right when she told us that we had probably already learned most of what was being taught. That was okay, though. I enjoyed being ahead in all of my classes.

"Hey, Brian. Wait up," a kid called after me as I was leaving the science classroom and heading out to the courtyard to meet Lisa. We were going to walk home together to the little bungalow Dad had rented on the beach.

"Hi," I said, turning around.

"I'm Bob Bradford," he said.

I stuck out my hand. "I'm Brian Chaffier," I said.

"How do you like school so far?" he asked. "Mrs. Hulet tells me you're interested in the goggling team. I'm captain and we could use another good swimmer. I'll wager you've done a lot of swimming, living on a boat and all."

"I sure have," I said. "When can I start?"

"This afternoon if you like. I'll take you down to practice and introduce you to the team."

I grinned and looked at his slight build. He was just a little shorter than me, probably about 5'5", with very tan skin and dark, curly hair.

"I don't know much about this place," I said as we chose a table and sat down to wait for Lisa. "I've only been ashore one day."

"No problem, Brian," Bob said. "I'll be your guide. Right now. Today."

"Thanks," I said.

"Isn't that your sister coming over?" Bob asked, pointing across the lawn. "She looks a little like you."

"Lisa has blond hair, I have brown. I'm tall, she's short. Yep, we're a perfect match," I joked. "Who's that with her?"

"Melanie Attwater. She's a good friend of mine," Bob said. "We can show you both around the island."

After I let Mom know that we'd be looking around the island with Bob and Melanie, the four of us headed off to the beach. On our way, we passed through downtown Victoria, named after Queen Victoria of England. There was even a statue of her in the town center, along with a miniature version of England's Big Ben clock. From the tower, roads radiated in all directions. Bob said you could travel anywhere on Mahé by starting at the clock.

"The town of Victoria is pretty small," Melanie said. "You can walk everywhere. Let's turn here and show Brian and Lisa all of the Chinese and Indian shops, Bob."

"Neat," Lisa said as we walked down the busy, narrow street. Melanie told us that the Seychelles had lots of immigrants from different places, like China and India. The tin-roofed buildings on either side had wide verandahs and were stocked with local handicrafts. We saw hand-carved domino sets, large leather belts, and elaborate foulards—a kind of turban tied on the head with a knot at the back. Then we passed through the vegetable market where old men played cards while they waited for customers.

"Matouloumba," Bob said.

"What?" I asked. "That sounds like some kind of magic spell."

"No, matouloumba is a popular card game. I'll teach you sometime."

"Okay. There sure is a lot to learn about this place."

An old bus rambled by. We hopped on and rode the Saint Louis trans-island road for about two miles, then got off at Beau Vallon beach.

A few minutes later we stood looking at a long bay with crystal clear water. White sand and a fringe of tatamaka trees lined the shore. The water was so calm it looked like glass.

"There's the team," Bob said. "Let's go. I want to tell them I'll be a little late."

The four of us hiked, single file, down the path to the beach. Besides the swim team, there were scuba divers farther out, a couple of water skiers, and several people riding what looked like surfboards.

Bob ran over to where the swimmers were practicing and talked to a tall guy. He pointed over to us. When Bob came back, Lisa said, "I could sure use a drink of something. All this exploring has made me thirsty."

Bob reached over for his pack and pulled out some bottles of soda. "I think I can take care of that," he said and handed them around.

"You really thought of everything," I said.

"Fail to plan, plan to fail," he replied. "That's my motto."

While we were drinking our sodas, a couple guys from the swim team came over to us and we started talking.

"So your dad's looking for the Buzzard's lair," Max, one of the guys on the team, said after Bob introduced us. "Your dad is famous. The whole town is talking about how long it will take him to find the treasure."

"Yeah, the Buzzard's almost like family," I told him, "Dad's really into it. He's been planning this trip for a while. He thinks it might be the greatest treasure he's ever looked for."

"I've lived with the legend of the Buzzard my whole life, too," Melanie said. "Cruise-Wilkins was my dad's cousin. My father worked with him in the early '60s."

"Really?" Lisa said. "That's cool. So you must know a lot about the clues and stuff."

"Aw, everybody on the island knows about the clues," Bob said. "The Savys were relatives of mine. But we don't think about the treasure much. No one has much hope that the treasure will ever be found."

"I wouldn't be too sure of that," Lisa

answered. "My dad's pretty persistent."

"Well, good luck to him," Max said. "He'll need it."

"What did he mean by that?" I asked Bob after Max had swum off toward the buoys at the end of his lane.

"Nothing. Just that we've seen a lot of people search and everyone has come up empty-handed."

"Not Stephen Chaffier," Lisa said proudly. "Dad always finds what he's looking for."

"I hope so," Melanie said.

"I actually don't," I remarked.

Everyone looked at me strangely.

"Well, I *do*," I explained, "but I hope it takes a long time. Then we'll get to stay here."

Bob grinned. "Well, I hope that treasure stays hidden for a long time, too!"

CHAPTER 3
A Disappearance

"MOM, Dad," I called as I entered the front door of our rented house a little while later. "We'd like you to meet our new friends."

"We're in the bedroom, Brian. Come on in," Mom answered.

I led the way through the small sitting room, past the kitchen and into my parent's bedroom. Lisa and I each had a tiny bedroom across the hall.

Dad was leaning over his duffel bag on the bed and Mom was handing him a stack of folded clothes when we entered. It seemed weird to have Dad packing while the rest of us still had some things to unpack.

"This is Melanie Attwater and Bob Bradford," Lisa said. "Melanie, Bob, meet our parents, Margeaux and Stephen Chaffier."

"Pleased to meet you," Bob said.

"Welcome to Mahé," Melanie added.

"Hi kids," Dad said, smiling at them.

"How was your first day at school and your

tour of the island?" Mom asked.

"Great!" I told them. "I'm going to join the swim team."

"How about you, Lisa?" Dad asked as he continued to pack his bag.

"My day was just fine. All the girls are really nice and I've already been invited to a party at Melanie's house on Friday night."

"I'm sure that will be fun," Mom said.

While they were talking I suddenly realized what Dad was doing. He was packing!

"Dad, are you leaving already?" I asked, my voice rising a notch. "I thought you were going to take it easy for awhile."

"Yeah, I was. I mean, I am. I'll rest after I check out the locations of the clues I know about," Dad told me. "I'm going to take a couple of the guys up into the mountains and . . . "

"We haven't even been here 24 hours and you're already getting ready to leave!" I said. "It's not fair."

"Brian," Mom said softly, "I don't think this is the time to discuss this."

I stared at my dad, not caring what Bob or Melanie thought. It was true, I had suspected something like this might happen. I had even told Lisa that treasure hunting was in Dad's blood and he would never stop. But I had hoped I was wrong. Now, it seemed, I was more right than ever. Wouldn't we ever have a normal family, one that stayed at home and did stuff together?

"Don't worry, Brian," Dad said. "We'll just look around to see what we're up against. Then I'll be back, and I promise that I'll take it slow after that. Okay?"

"I guess," I said, but I didn't believe for one minute that Dad would slow down. But what could I do about it? Dad was a treasure hunter. There wasn't any treasure in our living room, so he had to go find it where it was.

A few minutes later when we were saying good-bye to Bob and Melanie, Bob said, "It must be pretty difficult not having your dad around very much."

I tried to smile. "Yeah, well, it's his job to go look for treasure, I guess," I answered.

"Tell you what," he said. "I'll try to keep you and Lisa so busy that you won't notice your dad is gone. All right?"

"It's a deal."

* * * * *

Over the next two weeks, I almost forgot about my dad being off on a trip. There was so much to do. I started working out in the afternoons with the swim team. The school took our pictures for the class directory. And every spare minute we explored the area with Melanie and Bob. We hiked in the jungle, checked out the tidepools and shinnied up the long, curved trunks of the palm trees. It felt as if we had known Melanie and Bob all of our lives, not just a couple of weeks.

"I really like it here," I told Bob one day at lunch. "Mahé is like a tropical paradise."

"Sailing around and visiting strange places must be fun, too," Bob said. "I've only been off Seychelles once since I was born and that was only to Madagascar."

"Yeah. I guess you always want what you don't have," I said thoughtfully. "I like sailing and I'm sure I'd miss the ship if we lived on shore permanently. But for now, living on land is a vacation for me—except for Dad being gone." He had returned from his first trip and had gone off on another one a few days later.

"I know I'd miss my dad if he were gone a lot," Bob answered. "But I've got a job for you. It'll take your mind off your dad being gone."

"What's that?"

"Student directory. You know how they took our pictures last week? Well, Melanie and I and a couple of other kids are helping organize them for the directory. We're supposed to look at the proofs of the pictures this afternoon. Melanie is going to ask Lisa

33

if she wants to help, too."

"Sure, I'll help," I said. "I'm getting a big charge out of being in a student directory at all. We've never stayed in one place long enough to go to a real school, let alone have our pictures taken for a directory."

"Must be difficult not having to go to school," Bob joked. "So, anyway, meet us in the photography room after your last class."

The bell rang signaling the end of lunch period.

"I'll see you there," I told Bob as I headed off in the opposite direction to my math class.

After school I met Lisa in the courtyard as usual. We both started talking at the same time.

"Bob invited me to—"

"Melanie invited me to—"

We started laughing. "The student directory?" I asked.

Lisa nodded.

It didn't take us long to find the photography lab, which was around in back of the school. Together we headed out the front entrance. But as soon as we rounded the corner we found a huge crowd of people.

Two island police cars were parked outside the school, their red lights flashing. I saw Bob talking to one of the officers and waving his arms around frantically.

"What happened?" I asked Max, one of the

guys I knew from the swim team.

"I don't know," he said in a worried voice. "Melanie Attwater has disappeared. No one has seen her since the middle of the afternoon, and Bob found some of her things in the photo lab. The place was torn up, as if there had been a struggle."

"I-I don't understand," I stuttered. "What could happen to anyone in a place like Mahé?"

"I don't know," Max replied, "but the police look worried." He nodded toward the police cars. One policeman was writing down what Bob said in a notebook and the other was talking into his radio microphone.

"I don't like this," Lisa whispered. "Melanie knew she was meeting us in the photo lab. It isn't like her not to show up."

I saw that Lisa had tears in her eyes. I put my arm around her shoulder and said, "I'm sure nothing bad has happened. There's probably a good explanation for all of this. I bet Melanie will be back home by dinnertime."

But my voice sounded hollow, and I wasn't sure I really believed what I was saying.

After a few minutes, Bob came over to us. The look on his face didn't make us feel any better. "The police sergeant asked me to tell him everything I could. I think he's going to order a search of the island."

"Oh no!" Lisa exclaimed.

"He says it's just a precaution," Bob added. "It doesn't mean there's anything wrong."

"I think something's happened," Lisa said. "I just have a feeling."

Bob didn't say anything.

After a few more minutes, the police sergeant made an announcement over his car loudspeaker. "There will be a very thorough investigation," he said. "We'll be questioning her friends. For right now, I suggest all of you go home. We'll get this sorted out soon."

The crowd started to melt away. All of the kids were talking in low voices about Melanie. I know they all felt the way I did. It was hard to believe that someone would just disappear from this quiet place. But if Melanie really was all right, why couldn't anybody find her?

That night on the television news, they showed a picture of her and asked anyone with any information to call the police department.

I couldn't eat or sleep. It felt awful not being able to do anything or take any action. Just sitting there, waiting for news of her made me feel crazy. I had been so happy to finally have some friends in a place that felt like a home. And now something like this had happened.

I wished Dad were home.

CHAPTER 4
The Next Victims

"**M**OM, I think we should call Dad on the radio," I said the next morning when we were eating breakfast. "We should tell him what happened to Melanie, don't you think?" Melanie's mother had called us in the morning to say there was still no news and that the police had decided to treat the disappearance as a kidnapping.

"I don't know what your father could do to help," Mom said, "but we haven't talked to him in two days. Why don't we give him a call?"

Lisa's eyes were still red from crying the night before. "Maybe if he were here, he and the crew could help the police find her. He's had a lot of experience hunting for lost things."

Mom answered, "I'm sure the police are doing everything they possibly can."

"I'm so scared," Lisa cried. "What if she really was kidnapped?"

Mom put her arm around Lisa and said quietly, "We have to think positively. Maybe they'll find her today."

"I hope so," I said, turning to look out the window at the ocean. I blinked back my own stinging tears. "I like living on land. But life was a lot simpler when we only had to deal with ourselves."

Mom got the shortwave radio out and turned on the switch to send a message. She held the microphone up to her mouth and used the code names for Dad's group and us. "Buzzard's Treasure, this is HQ, do you copy? Buzzard's Treasure, this is HQ, do you read me?"

We listened to the static on the open channel for a few minutes, then tried again.

"He must not be at his base camp or else they're hiking around in a cave and have no reception," Mom said as she replaced the microphone in its cradle.

I picked up the transmitter and tried again with the same results—empty static. I kept trying until it was time to go to school. "Hey, wait a minute. Did Dad take everyone with him, or are some of the crew staying on the ship as they normally do?"

"Joe and Manuel stayed on the ship," Mom said. "Dad wanted someone close to the files in case he needs more information while he's in the field."

38

"I'll try calling them and see if they have any ideas."

Mom and Lisa went off to the kitchen and I dialed the frequency for the ship's radio. "This is HQ calling *Buzzard's Bounty*, do you read me?" I asked, then waited for a reply. No one answered.

"I think not being able to reach anyone is really weird," I told Lisa on the way to school. "I mean, what if I were Dad calling the ship for important information and no one answered."

"It is strange, isn't it," Lisa mused. "Joe hardly ever leaves the ship, except to shop for food."

I looked out toward the harbor. "It's like everyone we know is disappearing."

At school that day, the mood was really tense. The only thing people talked about was Melanie's disappearance. Bob said the police were at his house until about 11 o'clock the night before asking questions about her. He looked pretty tired.

Lisa and I went straight home from school because we wanted to try to get in touch with Dad again. But when we walked in the door, Mom told us that she had been trying all day.

"I think it's weird that Dad didn't come back to camp even once all day," I said at dinner. "And why aren't Joe and Manuel answering on the ship? I think I'll row out there after dinner and check it out."

But a storm blew in after we finished dinner and I couldn't make it out to the ship. So Lisa and I sat by the radio all evening, trying to make contact with either Dad's group or the ship. No one answered.

* * * * *

The phone rang the next morning when we were eating breakfast. Lisa and I looked at each other.

Mom answered and listened. The look on her face told us it was bad news.

"Did the police find Melanie?" Lisa asked anxiously when Mom hung up.

Mom shook her head. "No, Lisa. This time it's Bob Bradford. He's missing, too. That was his mother."

"Bob!" I yelled. Then I took a deep breath. "What's going on? Maybe he just went to look for Melanie. He said he wished he could do something to help."

"The police don't think so. Mrs. Bradford says that it looks like someone grabbed him. The police found his backpack on a trail last night. There were signs of a struggle."

I sat down hard on one of the kitchen chairs. "What's going on? Who would want Melanie and Bob?"

"I think the police are worried that the kidnappers will take more children," Mom explained. "They're asking everyone to go to school today so that they can question and protect them. The parents are supposed to escort their children to and from school."

"How soon do we have to be there?" Lisa asked. "At least talking to the police will feel like we're doing something, not just sitting around."

"I can't believe this is happening," I said. "I think we should try calling Dad again."

We tried, but again all we heard was static. I knew I shouldn't be worried. Sometimes Dad got involved in a search and forgot to check in. He always checked in, eventually. But this time, not being able to get hold of him bugged me. We didn't have time to wait. With all of the strange things going on, I couldn't help wondering if he was in trouble too.

Going to school and listening to the police try to make everything sound as if it were going to be fine didn't make me feel any less worried.

"We have to do something," I whispered to Lisa when we were finished talking to the police. "But what?"

"I have an idea," she whispered back. "Mom isn't going to be here for a little while to escort us home. Let's go over to the photography room where we can talk. That was the last place we were supposed to meet

41

Melanie and Bob. Maybe we'll find a clue there."

"I don't know, Lisa," I replied. "Do you think it's safe? Besides, I doubt if we'll find anything," I added, shaking my head. "Remember, we never had the meeting with them, so why would there be a clue in the photography room?"

"We'll be careful. And who knows if we'll find anything? But we have to start somewhere," Lisa said.

Cautiously we left the courtyard where the police still had several people left to interview. We slipped through the back door to the office and out the front door without being seen.

"So far so good," I said. "I feel like a spy."

"Shh!"

We jogged along the side wall of the classrooms around to the back of the school. Beyond the grassy play yard, the palm woods began. Past the palms, the land sloped upward into foothills covered in dark forests. Above the forests, granite peaks marched in a rugged line southward with the great bulk of Mount Trois Freres rearing its rocky head higher than the rest.

No one was around as we opened the door to the photography room and stepped inside.

We stood in the dark, catching our breath. We could just make out the outlines of the desks and tables in the center of the room. Suddenly my eye caught a movement in the back of the room.

"Did you see that?" Lisa hissed, grabbing my arm.

I felt along the wall next to the door for the light switch, found it, and turned it on.

The shadows disappeared. The movement we had seen had been the flutter of dark curtains at the window—the open window.

"Do you think someone was just in here?" Lisa wondered, her eyes wide with fright.

"There's no one in here now," I said, looking around. "There's no place to hide. It was probably just the wind blowing the curtain."

Lisa walked over to the big table in the center and pointed to the haphazard pile of photo proof sheets for the student directory. "Here's all of the stuff for the meeting, just as Melanie and Bob left it," she said as she sat down in a chair and began flipping through the sheets of photos.

"I wonder if we'll ever have a student directory now," I said.

"I wish Melanie and Bob were back, safe," Lisa declared. "I really miss them."

"Me, too." I looked through the photo sheets, which weren't in any particular order. "It's kind of strange, don't you think, that these are so messed up? Bob's so organized. You know, 'fail to plan, plan to fail.' I just

43

can't see him leaving them spread out all over the table like this, especially if he was getting ready for a staff meeting."

"Hmm, you're right," Lisa said. "I wonder what it means."

I picked up the proofs from one of the piles. They were the As and Bs. "Lisa, look at this," I hissed. "Here are Melanie's and Bob's pictures. They've been circled on this proof sheet!"

We looked at each other and back down at the pictures. "What does it all mean?" Lisa asked. "D-do you think the kidnappers circled their pictures?"

"I don't know."

"Are any other pictures circled?" Lisa asked.

"I was just wondering the same thing my—" I turned the page to the Cs. My hand froze in midair and I dropped the page.

"What's wrong, Brian?" Lisa asked. "You look like you've seen a ghost."

I swallowed hard. "I found two more pictures circled," I said slowly.

"Whose?"

I passed the page to her. "See for yourself," I said, my voice shaking. "First Melanie Attwater, then Bob Bradford, and now Lisa and Brian Chaffier. I think we've found the pattern. It's alphabetical order—and we're next!"

CHAPTER 5
The Sound of Silence

"WE have to tell the police!" Lisa cried. "We have to get some protection before it's too late!"

"Come on!" I said, heading for the door, the photos in my hand.

"Be careful," she warned. "They could be watching us right now."

I couldn't help the shiver that ran down my spine as I turned out the light. Cautiously, I opened the door to peer outside.

"I don't see anyone," I said in a low voice. It wasn't until we had both stepped outside and started down the side of the building that I saw the shadows.

Lisa saw them at the same time. She gripped my arm and pulled me back. People were waiting just around the corner of the building, but their shadows fell out where we could see them.

I leaned close to Lisa's ear. "It could be kids

or teachers," I suggested softly.

Lisa was already pulling me back. "Look," she pointed to the air above the shadows. "Smoke. No one is allowed to smoke on the school grounds."

Slowly, trying not to make any noise, we inched our way back to the photography room. Once inside, we didn't bother to turn on the light.

"The window," I suggested. "We'll go into the jungle and hike to our house to tell Mom. She can call the police."

"Okay," Lisa said. "Be quiet."

I nodded.

We looked out the window for a long time, studying the trees behind the school for any sign of movement. Finally we eased out of the window and sprinted across the grass to the shelter of the woods. Behind a clump of coconut palms, we studied the school until we had caught our breath. No one had moved.

"I think we gave them the slip," I said. "Let's head for home."

"I'm with you," Lisa said. "How soon do we sail?"

I had to smile. Home on the high seas had never seemed so inviting.

We walked quickly along the path keeping watch for anything strange up ahead. My eyes got tired of trying to concentrate on every detail. I had almost begun to feel safe when, about a hundred yards from home I felt the hair on the back of my neck begin to prickle. I held out my hand to stop Lisa.

"Slow down," I whispered, looking through the trees to the house. "I've got a funny feeling." My eyes scanned the trees, but I couldn't see anything. I sniffed the air, but all I smelled were tropical flowers and sea salt. I tried to stop breathing and listen, but all I could hear was the wind.

Still, I couldn't shake the feeling that we were walking into a trap. Everything was too quiet.

That was it! The normal sounds of the woods were absent. No birds cried out, no lizards rustled in the grass, no snakes slithered through the underbrush.

Then, up ahead, I heard a twig snap and saw a booted foot step out onto the path.

"Run!" I shouted. I spun Lisa around and yanked her back along the path.

"Get them!" I heard a man's voice yell behind me. "Get the little brats!"

I didn't bother to look. I knew there were at least two of them from the loud crashing noises they made as they chased after us. It seemed like bad guys were everywhere.

We ran for all we were worth, zigzagging between the trees, leaving the path and leaping over fallen palm trunks and piles of debris, trying to put as many obstacles between us and them as we could.

It was working. Behind us the shouts and curses were becoming fainter.

"Brian," Lisa panted as she ran beside me and we jumped over another dead palm together. "I can't run much farther. If we climbed a tree they might not see us."

"Good thinking. But we have to get far enough ahead to give us time to climb."

"Over there!" Lisa pointed to a grove of tall palms that towered above flowering flame trees and smaller evergreens and breadfruit trees.

"Lead the way!" I said.

We charged ahead, then swerved back, using a fallen tree trunk as a bridge. We chose the two tallest trees in the thicket, stuck our sandals in our teeth, and shinnied up the smooth, skinny trunks.

Climbing palm trees isn't the easiest job in the world, despite the practice we'd had with Melanie and Bob. We had barely made it above the canopy of evergreens and flame trees before we heard the men charging through the woods below.

I looked over at Lisa. She was holding on tightly to the trunk of her tree just a few feet above the bright red blossoms of an umbrella-shaped flame tree. She was biting her lip to keep from crying. I would have given her the thumb's up sign, but I couldn't risk letting go.

"Where did those fool kids go?" I heard a gruff voice below me shout. "How did we lose them?"

"They're probably hiding, the other man said. "Probably dug in a hole somewhere getting eaten by tarantulas."

That's it. Just keep looking for a hole and we'll be all right, I thought.

"I say we go back to the house and wait. They have to come home sometime," said the first guy.

For a second I thought I recognized his voice. But I couldn't be sure because it was muffled by the wind in the palm fronds over my head.

Suddenly I saw Lisa start to slip.

Hold on! I mouthed silently. She grabbed on tighter, but I knew she couldn't hold on much longer.

I knew I couldn't hold on much longer either. My arms were about to give out. Stinging sweat trickled down into my eyes.

Finally I heard the men leave. Luckily they made a lot of noise as they tromped back through the jungle toward our house.

Lisa started to slide again, this time unable to stop herself. I let myself down, too.

We dropped to the ground, half expecting that the men had played a trick on us and were waiting at the bottom. But we were alone.

"What are we going to do now, Brian?" Lisa whispered.

"We can't go home, that's for sure," I said. "I guess we're going to have to hike across the island and find Dad. He'll know what to do.

"You know what?" Lisa said. "I think we should go over to either Melanie's or Bob's house to see what's happening. We can call Mom from there."

"Good idea," I answered. "There's a path through the trees to Melanie's house that we could take."

"We'll have to wait until night and be very careful," she added.

"And if we see any sign of those goons, we're not hanging around to get acquainted," I told her.

"Deal," she said.

We made our way through the thickest part of the woods in the direction of Melanie's house. Getting there took us a long time because we studied every tree for about ten minutes before we walked to it.

"I'm starving," I said as we approached the Attwaters' backyard, which bordered the woods just like ours. "Maybe Mrs. Attwater will give us something to eat."

I looked around in the gray light of dusk. Everything seemed normal, including the sounds of the oncoming night. A white cat walked across the yard to investigate us.

Slowly we approached the Attwaters' back door and knocked softly. Mrs. Attwater answered.

"Come in, kids," she cried. "Your mother is worried about you. She phoned a while ago after she went to school to get you and you'd already left. She was so worried she called the police."

"We had to leave, Mrs. Attwater," Lisa said. "Someone chased us!"

As soon as the door closed behind us, Lisa and I each breathed a sigh.

Mrs. Attwater looked at us closely for the first time then. "What happened to you two? You're filthy! Did you say someone chased you? Tell me everything!"

"Well, we were in the photography room at school and saw the pictures for the student directory," I began.

"Melanie's and Bob's were circled and then we saw that our pictures were circled, too, so we knew we were next," Lisa said. "We think the kidnappers are taking kids in alphabetical order—Attwater, Bradford, Chaffier . . ."

"And there were these two men at the school," I added. "We saw their shadows, so we went out the window . . . "

"Wait a minute, slow down," Mrs. Attwater said. "In fact, sit down. I'm going to get Mr. Attwater so that he can hear this, too."

"I'm here," Mr. Attwater said, coming into the room. "Why didn't you go home?"

"We tried, but some guys were waiting for us on the path behind our house and they chased us into the woods. We climbed some trees and hid until they gave up. They said they were going back to our house to wait for us again," Lisa told them. "We can't go home. But we have to warn Mom!"

"Then you'll have to stay here," Mrs. Attwater said. "It's the safest place for you. I'll call your mom." She picked up the phone and dialed the number I'd written on a piece of paper in case I forgot it.

"But what if they're watching your house, too?" Lisa asked as Mrs. Attwater talked to Mom.

"We want to go find our father," I explained. "We haven't been able to get in touch with him and we're worried. Besides, he'll be able to help find Melanie and Bob."

"But we came here first to see if you'd heard anything," Lisa added.

The Attwaters looked at each other. "We've

received ransom notes from the kidnappers. So have the Bradfords," Mr. Attwater said. "It seems the kidnappers are after the Buzzard's treasure!"

"The Buzzard's treasure?" I exclaimed, astounded. "But that's our father's project. What does the treasure have to do with Melanie or Bob?"

"Didn't the kids mention that both of our families are connected to the Buzzard also?" Mrs. Attwater asked.

"They did say something when we first met them," I said, "but I forgot all about it until now. What was the connection again?"

"Reginald Herbert Cruise-Wilkins was my cousin," Mr. Attwater said "In fact, I came here with him in 1960 to help him search for the treasure. After he died, I decided that I liked Mahé enough to stay."

"And the Bradfords?" Lisa asked.

"The Bradfords are direct descendants of the Savy family, the first owners of the land where the treasure is supposed to be buried," Mrs. Attwater said. "So, you see, the kidnappers are after secrets that they think we have for finding the treasure."

"I guess the alphabet kidnapping theory was wrong. It was the Buzzard's treasure that they wanted all along," Lisa said.

"What did the ransom note say?" I asked.

Mr. Attwater smiled grimly. "We've got three days to give them the information about the Buzzard's treasure. They say that Melanie is safe—for now."

"But we don't have any secret information to give them," Mrs. Attwater added. "And the note said if we go to the police, they'll . . . they'll . . ."

She couldn't go on and Mr. Attwater put his arm around her. She sobbed on his shoulder. "They say we'll never see Melanie alive again if we don't do what they say," he told us.

We were quiet. Mrs. Attwater's sobs were the only sound in the room as the darkness closed in around us. Finally she said in a hoarse voice, "We only know what everyone else on the island knows. We would have searched for the treasure ourselves long ago if we knew anything. We're helpless . . ."

"And who's to say they won't try to kidnap us, too," Mr. Attwater said, his voice rising. Suddenly he slammed his fist on the table. A lamp fell off the table and shattered with a crash.

Then there was nothing but silence.

CHAPTER 6
On The Run

"**O**H no!" Lisa said suddenly, looking frightened. "I just thought of something. Since the kidnappers are after the Buzzard's treasure—they must have Dad, too!"

"We don't know that," I said, trying to push the thought from my mind.

"He didn't answer his radio," Lisa reminded me. "I'm really worried."

I took deep breaths to try to get hold of myself. I was starting to feel panicky. Kidnappers were after us, they probably already had our dad, and we couldn't even get to our mom because they were watching our house. Where would it all end?

"We have to get to him," I told her, standing up. "And according to the ransom note we only have three days." Then I asked the Attwaters, "Do you have a map of the island and a compass?"

"We're not letting you head off on your

own," Mr. Attwater said firmly. "We're going to call the police and have them take you back over to your house."

"But what about Mom?" Lisa cried.

"Don't worry, the police will know how to handle it," Mrs. Attwater said.

"Are you going to go to the police with the ransom note?" Lisa asked.

"It's hard to decide what to do," Mr. Attwater said with a deep sigh. "They say they'll hurt the children if we do go to the police. But the police are the only ones who can find them. I'm not . . ."

Just then the doorbell rang.

All four of us stopped talking and stared at the front door. Mrs. Attwater raised her finger to her lips and walked to the door. Without opening it, she called, "Who is it?"

"Constable Chris Martin of the Island Police!" a deep voice called back.

"Just a minute," she said.

Good, the police, I thought with a sigh of relief. *Just in time!*

But Mrs. Attwater started shaking her head violently. She walked quickly back to the kitchen. "Get out of here fast!" she whispered to us. "I don't know who's out there, but it's not Constable Chris Martin."

"H-how do you know?" I asked. This was getting too weird.

Mr. Attwater had a strange look on his

56

face. It's pretty scary when you know adults are starting to get frightened. Then you know what you're worried about is for real. I felt my hands shaking, and I couldn't make them stop.

Mr. Attwater spoke very slowly, as if he were trying to figure out what it meant himself. "We know Chris Martin," he whispered in a shaky voice, "from our church. Everyone calls her Chris, but her real name is Christine. The person at the door is a man!"

My eyes widened. I looked at Lisa and knew she was thinking the same thing I was. *When were we going to get to stop running?*

Mrs. Attwater said, "I don't know where the real Chris Martin is, but . . . "

The voice from the front door shouted again. "Open up, do you hear? This is the Island Police." Then the person who shouted started kicking the front door.

"Coming," Mrs. Attwater called.

Mr. Attwater pulled us close to him and said, "Listen very carefully to me. Go into the woods. Take this compass and map and go north until you get to the foot of Morne Seychellois, the highest mountain on the island. Wait for us at the shelter house on the southern slope, but stay out of sight. We'll get to the real police and join you there. We'll delay that man at the door as long as we can.

Do you understand me?" He gripped my shoulders so hard it hurt.

Lisa and I nodded, too scared to speak. My hand was still shaking as I reached for the compass. I felt like I couldn't catch my breath.

"We're depending on you," Mrs. Attwater said. I saw tears in her eyes. "And so is . . . so is . . . M-Melanie. . . ." She broke down.

"Now go!" Mr. Attwater whispered. "Out the back door."

We heard the front door start to splinter. I grabbed my backpack and a box of crackers that was on the counter top. With a quick look around, Lisa and I sprinted for the woods behind the house.

"We have to move fast," I said when we reached the palm forest and stopped to catch our breath. "It won't be long before that fake policeman at the door finds out what happened and comes after us."

"After he's finished with the Attwaters," she added. "What do you think will happen to them, Brian?"

I couldn't say what I was thinking. "Don't worry, Lisa, they'll be okay," I told her instead. But the thought was booming inside my head like an explosion: If something terrible happens to the Attwaters, and they can't get to the police, we're all alone. It will be up to Lisa and me to find Dad and to save Bob and Melanie.

After the sun went down, it was pretty dark in the deep woods. I led the way along the path lit only by the moonlight filtering through the branches overhead. We stuck to the path for awhile because it was wide and easy to follow. Then we came to a road.

"We have to head north to get to the foot of the mountain where the Attwaters are going to meet us," I said. "But we can't take the road because it heads west here. The path probably isn't safe," I said, checking the compass by the moonlight. "We have to hike into the jungle. There's no other way."

"Can't we wait until morning?" Lisa asked. She sounded pretty close to tears. "We don't have any idea what could be waiting for us out in that jungle."

"Lisa, I know you're tired. I'm dead beat myself. But if we travel at night, we'll be that much farther ahead of those fake police."

"Or that much more lost," she added.

"Look, Lisa," I said, "I'm just as scared as you are, but I'm trying to do what's best for us and for Melanie and Bob."

"Don't forget Dad," she said softly. "Okay," she added taking a deep breath, "let's keep moving. I just wish we had a flashlight."

"We'll make it," I said, as much to bolster my own confidence as to convince Lisa. Sometimes it's hard being the big brother.

In the eerie half-light, gnarled trunks of trees looked like ancient trolls. The huge fruits clinging to the trunks of the cannonball trees looked like brown heads watching us as we stumbled over the thick underbrush.

It was hard to see the compass in the dark, but I knew we had to climb. Dad had said he was going to make his base camp in the forest on the steep slopes of Morne Seychellois. So the shelter house at the foot of the mountain was on our way. We knew each tired step took us closer to Dad's camp and our meeting with Melanie's parents and the police. But what would we find at the camp? And would the Attwaters be able to escape the fake police officer who was kicking in their door?

But before we could get to either place we had to go north through the jungle.

Long, curved branches stretched skyward in front of us. As far as we could see, both left and right and straight ahead, the strange, monstrous mangrove trees blocked our way. Each tree looked like it had a thousand trunks, like long, bony fingers reaching out to keep us from passing. Beneath them, the ground felt soft and spongy. I imagined myself sinking into quicksand. As hard as I tried, I couldn't get the thought of being pulled into the green, slimy mire by long, bony fingers out of my mind.

We walked for at least an hour through the nightmarish moonlight, not talking, just pushing our way past the dripping tangles of vines and leaves, listening to every odd sound. A night bird called just a few feet above my head and I almost jumped out of my skin. After a while, though, the night noises quieted down. The loudest sound was our own breathing.

Lisa was right behind me—or was she? I couldn't hear her footsteps. She hadn't said anything for a long time, and my heart was beating so hard in my chest that I couldn't hear her breathing in back of me. I turned around and she practically ran into me.

"Brian!" she shouted and her voice was swallowed up by the swamp.

"Sorry," I said. "I just hadn't heard you for a while. You okay?"

"As okay as I can be slogging through mud in the middle of the night. I'm about ready to fall asleep on my feet," she said.

"We'll stop and rest as soon as we get clear of the swamp," I told her. "We'd get soaked if we tried to sleep here."

"And who knows what kind of animals live here," Lisa said, peering into the murky gloom. "Boa constrictors, spiders as big as your fist . . . "

Just then I felt something brush by my foot. "Aaah!" I yelled as I jumped back. "What do you think that was?"

We heard something scurry into the underbrush. Whether it was a snake or rat or what, we couldn't tell.

"Let's get out of here," I said. "I'm tired, too."

Luckily, we only had to hike about fifteen more minutes before we found a clearing. The ground was drier and instead of the creepy mangroves, we were in a cinnamon and vanilla thicket. The moon shone brightly in the open area between the trees and we found a flat spot to lie down.

"I'm so tired, I don't even care if I'm sleeping on bugs," Lisa said as she flopped down.

I sat down beside her and scanned the edges of the trees for any sign of movement.

"Aren't you going to sleep?" she asked.

"In a little while," I said. "I'm still pretty wound up. You sleep and I'll keep watch."

Lisa yawned. "Wake me up in a couple of hours and then I'll watch."

"Okay." I put my hand over my mouth to hide my own yawn. "We should get started again before daybreak."

"Uh huh," Lisa mumbled. She was already asleep.

I watched her sleep for a few minutes, then lay down myself, lacing my hands behind my head for a pillow. I stared up at the stars, the same ones we used to navigate the ship on the ocean. I prayed that they would lead me to my father and that he would be safe and everything would be all right. But the stars were so cold and distant. They seemed to echo Mrs. Attwater's words to me and Lisa: "We're depending on you . . ."

The next thing I realized a strange hoarse cooing sound woke me up. It was the next morning at dawn. A flock of turtle doves was feeding on cinnamon berries in the thicket next to us. I sat up with a jerk and the birds flew away, startled.

Lisa was propped up on one elbow.

"Hungry?" I asked.

"Starving."

"Well, we've got pancakes and granola, fresh fruit, doughnuts and sweet rolls, bagels, bacon, orange juice—"

"Brian! Stop that!" Lisa shrieked.

"Oh, I'm sorry, I was reading from the wrong menu," I said, smiling. "Instead we have half a box of crackers—yum yum!"

We ate some of the crackers, which had gotten soft in the humid jungle, then got up and headed north. In a while the swamps gave way to forests of larger trees. Colorful birds darted among the branches.

"What do you think we'll find at Dad's camp, Brian?" Lisa asked when we sat down to rest around noontime.

"We'll find Dad looking at his maps. And he'll look up and see us and say, 'I was just on my way home, kids. To take it easy, just like I promised I would.'"

Lisa looked at me and said, "That's not really what you think, is it?"

I stared at the ground for a second. Then I said, "I don't know what we'll find. I'm trying not to think about it."

"Well, first we have to meet the Attwaters," Lisa answered. "They'll have the real Island Police with them and then we'll find out what's been going on."

"I hope you're right," I said.

She must have noticed something in the tone of my voice, because she asked, "Well, why wouldn't that happen, Brian? Is something wrong?"

"Umm, not exactly," I told her. "But this is the shelter house where we're supposed to meet them. And no one's here. No Attwaters and no police."

"They're not here!" Lisa cried. "Are you sure this is the right place?"

"I'm sure, Lisa. We followed the directions and the compass. This is the only shelter house at the foot of Morne Seychellois. If we go any farther, we'll start up the mountain."

Lisa looked around at the huge trees on all sides of the shelter house and then started to cry softly. I put my arm around her and blinked back tears of my own. I had never felt so helpless.

After a while, she said, "Do you think something happened to the Attwaters?"

"Well, they're not here. And it would only take an hour or so for them to get here by helicopter. We've been hiking for almost a day. I don't know what's happened to the police. They should be here by now."

"What are we going to do, Brian?"

"Well," I answered, "maybe we should wait here until morning, just to make sure they're not coming. Then, I guess we'll know we're on our own."

Lisa picked up a rock and threw it at a tree. Then she asked, "What's the good of waiting? We know they're not coming if they're not here by now."

I just shrugged.

"Isn't Dad's camp supposed to be around here somewhere?" she asked.

"Yeah, as far as I can tell," I said, checking my compass. "We'll start going uphill and we're heading north. The cloud forest must start pretty soon. Dad's camp shouldn't be far now. I'm sure we'll see the smoke from their campfire and hear their voices when we get closer to them."

She looked me in the eye. "Let's go for it, Brian," she said. "What else can we do? The Attwaters aren't coming. And I don't know if

Dad'll be there or not, but we have to find out."

I had to smile, even though things didn't look too bright at that moment. "You're something else, Lisa," I said. "One minute you're crying and the next you're ready to take on the world. Okay, I'm with you."

We headed off up the gentle slope to the north. The eerie cloud forest began almost immediately.

Wisps of fog slithered through the trees, moistening everything they touched. All the plants and trees were slick and slimy. Moss covered all the rocks and climbed steadily up the tree trunks. It was almost like the long wisps of fog were alive and searching through the trees for anything that didn't belong in the strange and ghastly forest. I felt like they were searching for us.

We made steady progress through the trees, skirting the larger piles of undergrowth and climbing over the smaller ones. After we had been climbing for a few hours, the sun started to go down again. Was it possible, I wondered, that just a few days ago we were in our own house, safe and sound, worrying about things like the school directory and the swim team?

Suddenly up ahead, I saw something red and yellow through the trees.

Lisa saw them too. "Look!" she whispered.

"There are Dad's tents."

Cautiously, we crept forward.

We stayed hidden in the woods beside the camp for a long time.

My legs ached from squatting in one position for so long. Nothing moved. The only sounds were the sounds of the forest. Finally we decided to approach the camp.

"No one's here," Lisa said after we had walked all around. "The camp's abandoned."

"Ransacked is more like it," I said. I pointed to a jumbled pile of supplies in the middle of camp. "Look, there's the radio, broken into a million pieces."

Lisa went quickly into each tent. "The sleeping bags are all here, and Dad's clothes," she cried from Dad's tent.

"But no maps?" I asked, following her into the tent. "If Dad were here, notebooks and maps would be everywhere."

We searched through the mess. Papers, clothes, and supplies were strewn everywhere. But I didn't see any of Dad's maps, or any of his notes on breaking the code of the Buzzard's parchment.

"What are we going to do?" I asked, after we had looked through every tent. "First Melanie, then Bob, and now Dad and probably the whole crew have disappeared. I wish I had never heard of the Buzzard and his treasure and his stupid clues!"

I sat down, held my head in my hands, and just stared at the ruins of the camp. For the first time I started to wonder if we were going to get out of this alive. Now that we knew something awful had happened to Dad and his crew, things looked darker than ever.

Lisa was quiet too. But then she asked, "What did you say, Brian?"

"Huh?"

"About the Buzzard."

"You mean that I wish I had never heard of him and his treasure?"

"Yeah, but what did you say after that?"

"Uh, I don't know."

"Don't you remember?" she asked with a strange look on her face. "You said you wished you'd never heard of his stupid clues!"

"So what?"

"Don't you see, Brian?" She was almost yelling now. "That's what we'll do! That's our plan! It was right under our noses all along!"

"I-I don't get it."

"The clues!" she cried. "We'll follow the clues ourselves. We have them memorized after all this time. I have a feeling the clues will lead us to Dad and whoever is behind all this."

Now I understood what she was getting at. "First the gravestone at low tide, then the compass point stone," I said.

"The bald mountain that cries and the

underground cave with the carving of a sarcophagus," she added. "Water flowing off the feathers of a duck. We can do it!"

"We'll find Dad and whoever kidnapped Melanie and Bob," I said. "Then we'll get the police and—"

"NOW!" a voice yelled.

Before I had a chance to react, huge arms wrapped around me from behind, pinning my arms to my sides and lifting me off the ground. The man turned me away so that I couldn't see Lisa, but I could hear her struggling just like I was.

"It's too bad you won't have time to go to the police," a voice behind me growled. "You'll be fish food and we'll be rich before anyone even knows you're gone!"

I twisted and turned, trying to get a look at the man who held me. With a surge of power I finally jerked around enough to stare into his cruel, shining eyes.

"Hawk!"

CHAPTER 7
Modern-Day Pirates

HAWK'S deep laugh rang in my ears. "You kids thought you were so smart, coming here. But we had you figured out all along. It was only a matter of time."

"Where's Dad?" Lisa demanded.

Hawk turned me around so that I could see Lisa and the man who held her prisoner.

"Chester!" I said. "You? Why?"

"Fifty million smackaroos!" Chester hooted. "We're not splitting a single dime with your father. This time, the treasure is all ours." I'd never seen Chester or Hawk act like this. It seemed that the thought of all that money had driven them crazy.

"Where's Dad?" I asked angrily.

"Isn't that touching," Hawk said with a snicker. "Don't worry, he's all right. We still need him. He hasn't been talking much lately," he added ominously, "but I think you two will be just the ticket to loosen his tongue."

Hawk squeezed me tight and I let out

a loud whoosh of air.

"Come on, Hawk," Chester said. "Let's take them to their dear daddy."

"By all means," Hawk said sarcastically. "I can't wait to see the happy family reunion!"

"You are a jerk, Hawk," I muttered.

"What was that?" Hawk asked politely as he put my feet down, then started shoving me forward. He grabbed the back of my hair and yanked hard.

"Uh, I said your plan will never work, Hawk," I said, scowling.

Chester and Hawk tied our hands, then pushed us in front of them along a trail that climbed the mountain and ended at a cave. A large man guarded the entrance. When he stood up, a huge key ring jingled from his belt. I recognized the sound from the night on the ship when I had heard voices. So I hadn't been imagining things!

"I see you found the little buggers," he snarled. "It's about time! Throw them in there with the rest of the scum!"

"Children," said Hawk, "meet Officer Chris Martin of the Island Police." He, Chester, and the big goon started laughing hysterically.

The guard who had pretended to be Chris Martin bowed and said, "I almost had you at the Attwaters' house. They stalled as long as they could, but I figured out what was going on. For your information, they send their apologies for not being able to meet you with the Island Police. They're, shall we say, unavoidably detained." Again the three of them started laughing hysterically.

"Melanie's parents better be all right!" I cried, clenching my fists. "If you hurt them, I'll . . . "

"Don't worry about them, tough guy," said the big guard. "You have enough to worry about right here. Besides, no one will find them until we're long gone."

Hawk shoved my head forward so far that I almost fell, then he pushed me inside the cave. Lisa tumbled in after me.

"Don't try to escape," Chester warned. "There's no way out the back of the cave and we're watching the front."

"Where's Dad?" Lisa cried.

"Back here," we heard our father call. "Stay low and walk about twenty more steps. You'll find us."

"Us?" I asked as I stumbled ahead toward a small light.

"Melanie and Bob are here, too," Dad said. "Be careful not to hit your—"

"Ouch!" I yelled, bumping into some low-hanging rock.

"Heads," Dad finished.

Our eyes adjusted to the cave's dim interior. A few steps farther, we turned a corner and saw Dad, Melanie, and Bob

72

sitting in a cavern with a candle perched on a stone table in the center.

"You all right?" I asked Melanie and Bob. "Everyone is so worried about you. The police are searching the entire island. Everyone in Victoria is in a panic."

"We're fine," Bob said. He raised his eyebrows. "Except for this bump on my head and cramps in my arms from having them tied up for so long, I'm doing great."

"I'm hungry and tired," Melanie told us, "but I'm surviving."

"What are you two doing here?" I asked, looking toward Melanie and Bob. "I mean, why would Hawk and Chester want to kidnap you two?"

"Hawk found out that both Melanie and I are related to people who knew something about the treasure," Bob answered. "So he figured we knew family secrets that could help him."

"But we don't have any special clues to give," Melanie said. "Whatever our relatives knew died with them years before we were born."

Then Lisa looked at Dad. "What happened?" Lisa asked. "You didn't answer your radio after Melanie and Bob disappeared. Then when their parents got the ransom notes about the treasure, we knew we had to reach you. Melanie's parents

73

were going to help us find you, but the fake police came to the door and—"

"Whoa, slow down," Dad said.

"Is it just Hawk and Chester?" I asked. "Or is the whole crew in on it?"

"Who is that big guy with the missing teeth and the tattoos?" Lisa asked.

Dad groaned. "He's the ringleader. He calls himself Blackie and claims he's a descendant of Blackbeard."

"Oh, right!" I scoffed.

"Chester and Hawk dreamed up this whole scheme one night," Dad continued. "They lost a bunch of money to Blackie in a poker game and Blackie talked them into this stunt to pay him back."

"What about Joe and Manuel and Luke?" Lisa asked.

"Hawk sent Joe and the rest of the guys off on a wild goose chase to Praslin Island and then jumped me once we were at camp."

"Why?" Lisa asked. "They've been with you on dozens of expeditions. Hawk is your first mate. They were your friends . . . "

"What's friendship compared to $50 million," Dad said. "Besides, they're jealous."

"Jealousy doesn't have anything to do with it, Captain!" Hawk shouted, shining a light in Dad's eyes. He had been standing outside the cavern listening to everything we said. "We're just tired of you getting all the credit for discovering treasures. We aim to grab all the glory on this one—and all the money."

"It won't work, Hawk," Dad said. "You can kill me if you want, but I'm not going to lead you to the treasure. I don't even know where it is."

"You're lying!" Hawk yelled as he shoved the light practically up Dad's nose.

"We're not planning to hurt *you*, anyway," Chester said, joining us.

"That's right," Blackie snorted as he came up behind him. "But the kids, now that might be a different story."

Dad sucked in his breath. "You wouldn't be so low as to hurt the kids . . ."

He started to get up, but Hawk shoved him down with a booted foot. It was the same boot I'd seen on the path in back of our house.

"I'm afraid we just might be so low, Captain," Hawk said. "If you don't lead us to the treasure, the kids might get hurt, one by one, and we'll make it look like you did it. The cops will think that all this treasure hunting finally pushed you over the deep end and you went crazy. They'll lock you up and throw away the key."

"We'll start with this one right here," Blackie said, grabbing Lisa and yanking her up by her hair. She kicked him in the shins, but he held her tight. He put his arm around her shoulders and bent her neck way over to the side. She let out a cry of pain.

Dad's face turned beet red and the muscles on his neck strained. "Leave her alone!" he screamed.

"Ooh, he's begging now," Chester crowed.

"Take us to the treasure," Blackie said sweetly as he pulled a little harder on Lisa's neck.

"All right, you slime," Dad said. "I'll take you to the treasure. Now let her go!"

Blackie released Lisa's head. She hurried to sit down next to Dad, her eyes wide and scared.

I let out the breath I was holding.

"We'll break camp in the morning. Sleep well," Hawk told us wickedly.

"Yeah, with a rock for a pillow," Dad snarled as soon as they left. "When I get my hands on them, I'm going to . . ."

"Dad," I whispered, "you've got to buy us some time."

"How am I going to do that?" Dad answered.

"I know we can escape," I continued in a low voice. "But we need time to plan."

"Shut up in there!" Chester hollered from the cave's entrance.

I lowered my voice even more. "Follow the clues you know. Even retrace your steps, but just go as slowly as you can. Make a few mistakes."

"Maybe a couple of us can get away and warn the police," Bob added softly. "These guys have to be stopped. You know that once they get the treasure, there will be no reason to keep us alive."

Melanie nodded. "If we can just get to the police . . ."

Chester appeared with a lantern, kicked over our candle, and scowled at each of us in turn. "Not another word!"

Dad nodded. "Yep, I'm about ready to turn in. You kids try to get some sleep now," he said as he glared at Chester.

Chester left, leaving us in complete darkness.

"Everybody okay with this plan?" Dad whispered into the inky blackness.

"I am," I said, disguising my voice with a yawn.

"Me, too," Lisa added.

The others agreed. Then we tried to get some sleep, but it was pretty hard with our hands tied behind our backs.

Before light the next morning, Chester came in and kicked me. "Get up!" he screamed. "You and Melanie cook breakfast!"

Food! I'd completely forgotten how hungry I was! I hadn't eaten anything in over a day.

"Uh, sure," I said groggily. "Could you untie my hands? I have trouble holding a spoon with my teeth."

Dad shook his head, warning me not to get Chester riled.

Chester took out a long dagger from the sheath at his belt. He grinned and hummed a tune as he turned me around. I felt cold steel at my wrist and gritted my teeth, waiting for the pain when he cut me. But he just sliced through the rope instead and walked out of the cave laughing.

I rushed over to Melanie and untied her. I was about to untie Dad when I heard Hawk shout, "Only the girl! Get out here and start cooking! The rest of you come out here where we can keep an eye on you."

We all trooped out of the cave and found Chester, Blackie, and Hawk sitting in front of a roaring campfire.

"You consider yourselves real modern-day pirates, don't you?" Dad said, easing himself down on a log.

I had to hand it to Dad, he was cool and appeared calm, even though I knew he was boiling underneath.

"We're even better pirates than the Buzzard," Chester chuckled. "He got caught!"

"You will, too. You'll end up just like the Buzzard," Lisa said, glaring at all three of them. "The bad guys always get caught."

Blackie laughed and stared right back at her. "Not if they don't leave any evidence," he hissed through his teeth.

CHAPTER 8
Counting Clues

"YOU would think those guys already were millionaires the way they order everyone around," Lisa said to me. "Fetch the water, carry the packs, cook the breakfast," she said.

"No talking in line!" Hawk shouted. "Just carry your loads and shut up."

I rolled my eyes. "He really is losing his mind."

"I agree," Lisa said. "I think Hawk is insane. He's really changed."

We were all walking on a trail that headed roughly south out of the camp. We had to carry all the stuff, while the "pirates" strolled along. We were leading them to the fourth clue.

Dad had already found the first two clues before he, Hawk, and Chester had hiked up into the hills. The cave where we were prisoners was the third clue. In it, Dad had found more carvings that matched the diagrams on the Buzzard's parchment. He had found that we had to walk two miles 160 degrees southeast, then one mile 260 degrees west southwest. There we were supposed to find twin peaks, joined together with a natural bridge.

We had been walking for three hours as slowly as possible when Chester finally got angry. "Where's the bloody bridge, Captain?" he demanded.

"It must be up ahead a ways still," Dad answered.

"I'll bet we're headed in the wrong direction," Hawk shouted.

"Check the readings for yourself," Dad said, offering him the compass.

"Just speed it up," Blackie ordered. "We don't have all day."

"I didn't know you boys were in such a hurry," Dad said calmly.

"Well, we are," Chester said, "so get a move on."

"That looks like the bridge right up ahead," Dad said, pointing to a rock pile between two tall peaks. The way the rocks were piled it really did look like a bridge—from far away anyway.

We hiked faster, then Dad took his time examining every boulder at the base of the natural bridge. I saw him walk past a large rock shaped sort of like a duck and something clicked in my memory. The carvings we were looking for were supposed to be like water rolling off the feathers on a duck.

Good for you, Dad, I thought. *Stall as long as you can.*

I looked around, trying to figure out if there was an escape route back to Victoria from the twin peaks, but I wasn't sure where the town was from there. Besides, there was nowhere to hide. The trees were sparser at the higher elevations. We'd have to wait until nightfall when we made camp again and try to slip away under cover of darkness.

"You're stalling, Chaffier!" Hawk said. "Even I know that the clue is carved on a duck. You walked past that rock twice without checking it out."

Dad looked at the duck-shaped rock as if seeing it for the first time. "You know, Hawk, you may be right. I guess I'd better have a look."

"Don't get smart with me!" Hawk shouted. Then he slugged Dad on the side of the head. Dad stumbled and came up mad, his fists clenched.

I took a step toward him. But Hawk already had his knife out, waving it around, ready to jab it at the first person who moved.

"Easy now, Hawk. Let's have a look at those markings, shall we?" Dad said, watching him carefully. "We're not going anywhere. We want to find the treasure as much as you do so that we can all go home."

"Yeah, and if you're nice to us, we may even cut you in," Chester said, smiling sweetly.

Blackie grinned, showing off his missing front tooth, then took his knife out and nonchalantly cleaned his fingernails.

"That's mighty generous of you boys," Dad said through clenched teeth. "Maybe I should have asked you to run the show months ago."

"Maybe you should have," Hawk said. "But we're running it now, and I say look at those markings!"

Dad bent down to study the rock and compared the markings on it to those on his chart.

"We have to hike between the peaks to that ridge over there," he said, pointing west, "then wait until sunset and watch for the spot where the setting sun last touches the tallest mountain—Morne Seychellois—in the spring. The Buzzard says that the point where the bald man—in this case, the mountain—cries for his lost love—the sun— is where we'll find the fourth clue."

"That's very poetic, isn't it?" Chester said,

pushing Dad forward. "Come on, we'll make camp before the sun sets and be ready for the tears to fall."

"Tears of gold," Hawk said, bursting into laughter and slapping his thigh.

Chester and Blackie laughed, too.

No one else thought the joke was funny.

Dad led the way again, over the bridge, through the mist-shrouded forest below where the sun didn't shine and the fog crept around us like ghostly fingers. Then we climbed back up again onto the rocky ridge.

We were picking our way along a steep, rocky trail when I heard the rocks slide away behind me. Bob had fallen!

"Ow!" Bob cried out from where he lay on the loose rubble, clutching his leg in pain. "I think I broke my ankle."

"Fat chance," Chester said. "We're not leaving you here. Get up."

"I can't," Bob said.

"Get up anyway!" Chester ordered.

Bob tried to put weight on his foot, but fell again.

"I'll help you," Melanie said, glaring at Chester. "Can't you see that he's hurt?"

"He's faking it," Chester said. "I'll bet if I pricked him with my knife, he'd move."

Bob finally stood up, leaning heavily on Melanie. His face was pale and he was sweating. He tried to take a step. "Aaah!" he yelled. "It's broken, you fools."

"Broken, my eye!" Blackie yelled, rushing back to Bob, his fist raised. "I'll show you broken!" He pulled his arm back to hit Bob and threw the punch, but stopped an inch in front of Bob's face.

"Gotcha!" Blackie shouted.

Bob had put his arm up to ward off the blow. But he stayed where he was, balanced on one foot and leaning on Melanie.

"If it's not broken, you're going to wish it were," Hawk threatened.

"This is as good a place as any to make camp and watch the sunset," Dad interrupted quickly. "I'll take a look at Bob's ankle while we're waiting."

"Thanks, Mr. Chaffier," Bob said, still keeping his eyes on Blackie.

"You girls make dinner," Hawk said, turning away from Bob as Blackie lowered his fist. "Brian, you set up the tent. You all are sleeping inside tonight."

I started to walk toward Bob.

"Now!" Chester ordered.

"Yes, sir!" I muttered sarcastically.

I counted to ten as I walked to my pack. Actually, it was Chester's pack, but he had made me carry it.

I counted to twenty as I loosened the

bungee cords from the tent and spread it out on the ground. One by one I fed the poles into the casings and curved them over to form the shape of a dome. The tent was only meant to sleep three people. The five of us were going to be very crowded that night.

Bob came hobbling over to the tent leaning on Dad's arm.

"Do you think it's broken?" I asked. Hawk was listening intently.

"No, I think he just twisted it," Dad said, looking at his former first mate. "He might be able to put some weight on it by morning."

"Good thing or we might have had to leave him here," Hawk drawled. "Under a rock."

"Go on inside the tent and rest, Bob," I told him softly. "Maybe if those goons don't see you, they won't think of a job for you to do."

Bob ducked into the tent and I continued to crawl around on the outside of it, trying to hammer the stakes into the rocky ground. The wind was coming up, shaking the tops of the palm trees and wafting the smell of cinnamon through the air.

"I'm hungry," Bob said, from inside the tent.

"I'm more mad than hungry," I said from outside the tent.

"How are we going to get away from these guys?" Bob whispered.

"I was just thinking the same thing," I answered. "Maybe if we can lull them into a false sense of security by doing everything they say, a couple of us can escape."

"When? Who?"

I looked up to see Chester watching me and banged my thumb with the hammer.

"Tonight," I whispered to Bob. "You and Melanie know the way, so you should go. How's your ankle, really?" I asked.

"Never felt better," Bob said.

He had done a great acting job—fooling even me. "You're sly," I said.

I turned my attention back to the hammer. I turned it over to the claw side and quickly jabbed a hole in one of the seams. Then I went back to pounding in stakes. "I'll bring you some food," I said. "You stay in the tent and moan occasionally to make them think you're really hurt."

"Aye, aye, Captain."

"Cut the pirate talk," I said. "I've had enough of pirates to last me a lifetime."

Melanie and Lisa had finished fixing the meal by the time I finished putting up the tent. Dad was sitting next to a tree, his hands and feet tied.

"The sun's going down," Dad called out. "I need untied so that I can hike up on that ridge and watch the sun touch bottom."

"Take your food and eat while you're watching" Chester said. "It's the last time you'll be out of the ropes tonight."

"Thanks," Dad said, as Chester untied the knot. He dug in his back pocket for the chart and started hiking for the ridge. I followed, with Chester and Hawk right behind. Blackie stayed in camp to guard the girls and Bob.

We reached the top of the ridge just as the sun dipped between the twin peaks. The big, orange ball stayed between them as if cradled in a giant's hand. Then it slowly slipped out of sight behind the bridge, shooting its last rays across the valley and onto the bald, gray precipice of Morne Seychellois.

A dark shadow line, like oozing blood, crept up the side of the mountain until only the top point glowed gold and red in the dying light.

"There it is, Brian!" Dad cried excitedly, almost as though he had forgotten about Chester and Hawk. "See the waterfall on the north side? I'll bet it only flows during the spring runoff."

I stepped closer and focused on the trickle of water, glinting silver against the golden light. "Wow!" I breathed, for a second, feeling the same joy of discovery. The way the shadows fell on the rocky face of the mountain I could almost see eyes, a nose, and a mouth.

"The bald man crying for his lost love," Dad said softly. "The Buzzard had quite an imagination. I have more respect for him every step of the way."

"How long do you think it will take us to hike up there in the morning?" Hawk asked.

"I don't know, a couple of hours," Dad said.

"Let's go back and get some shut-eye then," Hawk ordered. He shoved Dad ahead of him, holding the knife as a warning.

"Kind of takes all the fun out of a good treasure hunt, doesn't it?" Dad said to me.

I nodded. "It sure does."

CHAPTER 9
The Buzzard's Curse

"**W**HY do you have to tie us up?" Melanie complained to Hawk later that evening when we were ready to sleep.

"Yeah, it's hard to sleep with your hands behind your back," Lisa added as Chester yanked her ropes tight.

"Poor things. Maybe you'd like to go to sleep permanently?" Chester commented.

"You won't get away with this," I told them. "Besides, even if you do, the Buzzard's curse will get you."

"Curse! I'm not afraid of any curse," Chester answered with a laugh.

"Good thing," Dad said as he ducked into the tent. "Because there were a few incidents I didn't mention when I was telling you the legend of the Buzzard all these years."

There was silence for about a minute, then Hawk threw back the tent flap. "Get back out here and spit it out," he demanded.

"Well," Dad said, "I didn't want to worry you unnecessarily. They were probably all accidents. . . ."

"What accidents?" Hawk asked.

"Well, I told you that everyone who has searched for the Buzzard's treasure for the past 300 years has died before finding it."

"So?" Blackie said. "What's that got to do with us?"

"Probably nothing," Dad remarked after a brief pause. "I guess I just forgot to mention the ones who disappeared."

"Disappeared?" Chester asked.

"Well, there was an English missionary who left his church to follow the call of the Buzzard's gold. He told his family that he had found the final clue and that he would be back in the morning with the treasure. . . . "

"What happened, Dad?" I asked.

"He was never seen again," Dad told us.

"Really?" Melanie cried.

"And then there was an Australian scientist just twenty years ago who came here on an expedition for his university," Dad continued.

"And what happened to him?" Blackie asked sarcastically.

Dad dropped his voice to a whisper and looked directly at Blackie. "We'll probably never know. They found his skeleton washed up on the beach at high tide last year."

Hawk glanced at Chester. Neither of them said anything.

"I read about that scientist guy in the paper," Melanie commented. She shuddered. "They showed a picture and everything. The doubloon they found near the skeleton is in the Queen's Museum in Victoria."

"Oh yeah," Bob said from just inside the tent. "And remember that guy who was digging on the beach a few months ago? They found him one morning, dead, his eyes bulged open."

"They say he was scared to death," Melanie reported, "because there were no marks on his body and no signs of a struggle. But with his finger, he had drawn the head of a buzzard in the sand."

"That's enough!" Chester said. "Go to sleep, all of you! No more ghost stories. Tomorrow we've got work to do."

"Quit letting them get to you," I heard Blackie tell Hawk and Chester after we had gone into the tent. "They're just trying to rattle you."

Maybe the stories were working after all, I told myself. Chester and Hawk seemed more jittery than ever.

We all squeezed into the tent and tried to get comfortable, which is pretty hard to do with your arms pulled back as far as they can go and ropes biting into your wrists.

I scooted over beside Bob and whispered in his ear. "You have to escape tonight. Give me your hands, I'll untie you."

We sat back to back and I worked on the knots in his ropes. I nodded my head to Lisa. "Help Melanie," I whispered.

Untying their ropes seemed to take an hour, but finally Bob was able to pull his hands free. He untied his legs and then helped Lisa finish off Melanie's.

We listened, but all was quiet outside.

"Do you think they're asleep?" Melanie whispered.

I shook my head and leaned over to peek out the tent flap. "Chester's keeping watch, but he's starting to nod off. You've got to rip that hole larger in the back of the tent and crawl out."

"Let us untie you and we'll all go," Melanie said, reaching for my ropes.

"No," I said. "We would move slower as a group and be easier to find. Besides, the three of us can stay here and stall."

"Brian's right," Dad said. "You two know the island. You can alert the authorities. Meet us in Deadman's Cove, below the lookout cliffs, tomorrow night. I'll stall until then to give you enough time. Look for us near the feet of the waterlogged woman. There's supposed to be a cave under the sand at low tide."

"Don't waste any more time," Lisa whispered. "Get going. Good luck."

I handed Bob my compass and watched as he put his finger in the rip I had made with the hammer and pulled. The tearing noise sounded as loud as a gunshot in the silence. Quickly we all lay down, our hands behind our backs.

I heard Chester's footsteps and then his breathing as he lifted the flap and peered in to check on us. He walked around the tent and I held my breath. If he saw the rip in the seam, there was no telling what he would do to us. When his footsteps continued on around back to the fire, I exhaled slowly.

Using the glow of firelight through the side of the tent, Melanie reached over and started pulling threads out of the hole one at a time with her fingernails. Slowly, but surely, the rip lengthened, until finally it was big enough for a person to fit through.

"Wait!" I whispered. "Check on Chester first."

Bob looked out the front door. "He's asleep and so are Hawk and Blackie."

The fire was almost out and we could barely make out our own shapes in the darkness when Melanie and Bob finally squeezed through the hole.

"Be careful," Dad told them. "And whatever happens, keep going."

"Good luck," Bob said. "And if you have a chance to get away, do it."

We all nodded, then watched through the hole in the back of the tent as they tiptoed silently out of camp and faded into the night.

In the darkness, I crossed my fingers.

*   *   *   *   *

"Wake up!" Hawk bellowed the next morning at daybreak.

I blinked and came awake instantly, not remembering having gone to sleep.

"Wait until he sees that Melanie and Bob are gone," Lisa said.

"We'd better act surprised and we'd better do it now," Dad said.

I stood and stumbled out of the tent, my hands and feet still tied. "Where are Melanie and Bob?" I demanded. "What have you done with them?"

"I want my friend back!" Lisa yelled. "If you've hurt her, I'll . . . I'll . . . "

"Hurt who?" Hawk asked. "What are you talking about?"

"Where are the other two children?" Dad

asked as he emerged from the tent and stood up.

"They're in the tent, stupid," Blackie answered.

"They're not in the tent," Dad said, frowning. "And you know it!" He jerked his head in the direction of the tent flap.

"If this is a trick . . . " Hawk warned. "You kids come out of there," he yelled into the tent.

There was no answer.

"Cover me," he told Chester. Chester drew his knife.

Hawk unsheathed his machete from its carrying case on his belt and used it to open the tent flap. Then he stuck his head into the tent. He pulled it out as if he had seen a ghost.

"They're gone," he announced, narrowing his eyes and brandishing his machete. "There's a rip in the tent a mile wide. Obviously, you helped them escape," he accused Dad.

"How could we help them escape?" Dad asked calmly. "We were tied up. We're *still* tied up."

Hawk, Chester, and Blackie huddled together and whispered for a while.

"Don't you think you should go after them?" Dad called over to them.

"There's no time. They'll probably be swallowed up by the swamp long before they can get back to Victoria," Blackie said. "Besides, all this means is that we have to move faster. No more stalling, Captain. You lead us to the treasure tonight. Or else!"

Lisa and I stared at Dad. We were wondering the same thing. Could Melanie and Bob make it back to Victoria and warn the authorities before these sick treasure hunters found the treasure, finished us off, and made their escape?

"How about breakfast?" Dad asked.

You're cool, Dad, I thought. *That's for sure.*

"Forget breakfast," Hawk said. "Pack up and move out! Now!"

CHAPTER 10
The Nightmare Is Real

WE hiked up to the waterfall on the steep side of Morne Seychellois. There we located the carvings worn almost smooth by three hundred years of flowing water. From there we found three clues in a straight line, heading down off the mountain toward the unpopulated northern shore of Mahé.

One clue was a gigantic palm, which was no longer there. But Dad checked his diagrams and followed the drawings to an additional clue: the only granite boulder in the center of a swampy meadow.

We ate as we walked, and no one talked much. I knew every step closer to the waterlogged woman meant we were running out of time.

"Do you think we'll, you know, make it out of this alive?" Lisa asked me. "Do you think we'll ever see Mom again?"

"Don't worry, Lisa. We're not going to die," I assured her. "We'll figure a way out of this."

"I hope Melanie and Bob are safe," she said.

"They're probably on the way back for us right now." *I hope so, anyway.* That's what I was thinking, but I couldn't tell Lisa.

Tired and sweaty from swatting mosquitoes and trying to lift my soaked shoes and put them down one more time in the mire, I felt ready to give up, too. I hoped I never saw another treasure map and never hiked another step.

When we finally hiked around a steep hill and stood staring straight down at Deadman's Cove, I knew this would be over soon.

"Well, where is it?" Blackie asked, scanning the horizon and gazing down the 300 feet to the crashing waves below in the cove.

"We have to hike down to the beach to find the waterlogged woman and dig at her feet," Dad said wearily.

"The waterlogged woman?" Hawk screamed. "That's the very first clue! Chaffier, you've just taken us on a wild goose chase."

"That's not true!" Dad answered. "I had no idea the clues would lead back to the waterlogged woman. Ol' Buzzard must be laughing at us from his grave. It was Buzzard who lead us in a giant circle."

"So what are we waiting for?" Chester said, rubbing his hands eagerly. "Let's go."

Suddenly Dad swung wildly and knocked Chester off his feet. I launched myself at Hawk, but he was too fast for me. Steel flashed in front of my face and I threw myself to the side to avoid his blade. Lisa charged the fallen Chester, jumped on his back, and tried to kick him.

"Argh!" Chester groaned.

"I wouldn't do that, little lady," Blackie threatened. He had his beefy arm around Dad's neck, his knife pressed against Dad's throat. A drop of blood welled up where the blade pricked his skin.

"Get up, you fool!" Blackie yelled at Chester.

Chester threw Lisa aside and rose to his knees with a snarl. "Don't ever try something stupid like that again, Chaffier!"

"Come on," Hawk said. "It's getting dark and I don't want to be digging in the dark. Correction—I don't want *our friends* here to be digging in the dark!" He laughed obnoxiously at his stupid joke and the other two joined in.

We worked our way down the cliff, onto the sand, measured fifty paces, and stopped right where Dad and the others must have started two weeks ago. We all stared at the head and shoulders of a statue—a ship's figurehead that shipbuilders attached to the bows of their ships.

"Where's the last clue?" Hawk demanded, tapping the waterlogged woman on the head with his machete.

"Covered up by the sand, most likely," Dad said.

Chester tested the sharpness of his blade on his thumb. "I think you're leading us on a wild goose chase," he said.

"I have a new theory," Dad explained, ignoring Chester's comment. "And the markings on the granite boulder back in the swamp confirmed my suspicions," Dad said as he walked up the beach to a pair of oval boulders. "I think these boulders are the waterlogged woman's feet!"

Everyone just stared at him. "But what about the statue?" Chester growled.

"She's just a bust. She has a body and a head, but no feet. Two weeks ago we dug where her feet were *supposed* to be and found nothing."

I looked back at the woman. "Are you sure she doesn't have any feet?" I asked.

"Positive," Dad confirmed. He turned to the two boulders. "I think the Buzzard's treasure is near here."

Chester grinned. "Well, what are *you* waiting for. Start digging!"

"Come on, kids," Dad said, pulling the

shovels out of one of the packs.

Darkness fell, the full moon rose, and the tide moved out as we dug in first one place and then another. Finally, after several hours of backbreaking digging, my shovel struck something hard. It was stone.

I knelt down and wiped the wet sand away. I caught my breath as the moonlight revealed the stone face of a woman.

"Wow!" I whispered. "Another statue!"

"I didn't expect that," Dad said, dropping to his knees to examine the statue.

Lisa knelt beside him and they wiped the sand away from the statue's body. It was carved from stone and looked like a pure white pearl in the moonlight.

As we removed the sand from the statue's ankles, we noticed that they were braced right against the base of the two boulders which were shaped a little like shoes. She had no feet, only the rocks.

"So this is the real waterlogged woman," Dad said. "Let's dig at her feet."

The sand was wet as we dug around the base of the boulders, and a real pain to dig. But Chester and Hawk stood over us, their knives a constant reminder that this was no ordinary treasure hunt. Blackie kept a wary watch on the beach and the woods. Whenever I could I looked around, too, hoping that I would spot Bob, Melanie, and an army of police coming to rescue us. It had been almost 24 hours since they escaped. They must have reached the authorities by now. What could be keeping them?

We had dug nearly five feet down when Dad stopped to rest.

"Keep digging," Hawk ordered.

"More sand is going into the hole than coming out," Dad reasoned. "We don't even know if the cave mentioned in the clue is here."

Waves crashed onto the shore and pulled the sand with them when they receded. It must have been nearing midnight. I remembered reading that low tide was supposed to happen at close to midnight all this week.

"All right, I'll dig, but don't hold your breath," Dad said in disgust. He raised the shovel and struck it down hard, down through the soggy sand until it struck stone.

"I guess that's it," he said, leaning on the shovel. "A dead end."

Suddenly the sand beneath our feet began to shake. A deep rumble vibrated from below.

"It's an earthquake!" Lisa screamed, then dropped to her knees and covered her head in fear.

Dad started wobbling as the ground beneath him started to give way.

"Dad! Get out of there!" I shouted, but my

voice was drowned out by the rumble of crashing earth.

And then, before our startled eyes, Dad was sucked down into the ground. He disappeared, swallowed by the sand without a trace!

"Dad!" Lisa shrieked.

A huge hole had opened in the sand. Dad was nowhere in sight. Without thinking I jumped into the hole and landed in knee-deep water below. It must have been ten feet from the opening of the hole on the beach to the floor of the cave where I landed.

"Dad?" I yelled into the darkness.

"I'm here," Dad said, his voice muffled.

"Are you all right?"

"Yeah. I fell on a pile of sticks or something," he said.

As my eyes became more accustomed to the dark, I realized Dad and I were in a cave, just as I thought. The cave was a large underground room and smelled like seaweed and stale, musty air.

"Do you think this is the cave that Cruise-Wilkins talked about?" I asked in a low voice so the others on the beach couldn't hear me. "The one with the drawing of the sarcophagus on the wall? Do you think we're getting close to the treasure chamber?"

"I think we're mighty close," Dad said. "I just wish I could get the jump on those guys."

103

"What's going on down there?" Chester called into the hole. "Remember, we've still got your girl up here."

Dad sighed and put his hand on my shoulder. "I'm sorry for putting you two through all this," he said softly to me in the darkness.

I tried to smile at him, even though I knew he could barely see me. "I'm just glad we could be here with you, Dad," I said. "I hope we can help you."

I felt Dad's hand squeeze my shoulder.

"Throw down a light and a rope," he yelled to the men up above. "Come down and see for yourselves."

"Why don't we just jump them?" I whispered to Dad. "We could take them the second they come down the rope. We'll tie them up and leave them here until we can get the police."

"You can bet they'll be on guard for that kind of move, Brian," Dad told me. "They're smart enough to be ready for something like that. But what's worse, they're crazy. The thought of the Buzzard's riches has driven them over the edge. I don't trust them for a moment. Especially Blackie."

"But what are we going to do?"

"I guess we'll just have to strike fast when we have the chance," he told me.

"I'm ready when you are," I promised. I felt

104

around in the shallow water for one of the sticks that we fell on. I needed a weapon close by and ready. I grabbed a long, smooth one with a knob on the end.

"We're sending Lisa down first, Captain," Chester called from above.

"See what I mean," Dad said. "They aren't taking any chances. They have the rope. They have the light. Leaving us down here would be certain death as soon as the tide comes back in."

I gripped my club tighter as Dad called up to Hawk and Chester.

"Send the light down with her so we can catch her," he told them.

"Here she comes," Hawk called back.

We looked up to see Lisa, her foot in a makeshift stirrup, one hand gripping the rope and the other holding a flashlight. They let her down slowly into Dad's arms.

Lisa buried her face in Dad's shoulder. "What is this horrible place?" she cried.

"I don't know what it is, a cave of some kind," I told her. "But at least we have weapons." I lifted the stick to show her and she shined the flashlight on it.

But it wasn't a stick.

It was the leg bone of a human skeleton.

"Aaaah!"

We both screamed at the same time and our yells reverberated around the cave. I dropped the bone and looked down. Floating in the water all around us were hundreds of ghastly white bones.

I closed my eyes and opened them again. "This isn't a cave," I whispered. "It's a tomb, a pirate's graveyard!"

"The Buzzard probably left these guys here to guard his treasure," Dad added in a shaky voice.

"Whoa!" Chester said as he was climbing down the rope. "Okay," he called when his feet touched bottom.

Hawk followed immediately. "Ho, ho!" he said, looking at the floating bones. "Company."

Blackie stayed up on top, holding the rope.

Lisa whimpered on Dad's neck. "Don't put me down."

"I won't, sweetie," Dad said. "All right, you guys," he said, turning to his two former friends. "This is as far as I know anything about."

Dad shined the flashlight beam on the nearest wall. It was rock. "There's the picture of the sarcophagus on the wall. There's the carving of the head of a skeleton with a triangle on its forehead. These are the clues we've been looking for. The rest is up to you."

Dad started moving toward the rope.

"Where do you think you're going?" Hawk asked. "What about the twelfth clue? You said you had it all figured out."

"Nope," Dad said. "I said I had figured out a few words of the code. I'll tell them to you. 'To the sea. Riches. Fullest pleasure, true treasure.'"

"What's that supposed to mean?" Chester demanded. "Start looking around or else it'll be the end of you."

"Face it, boys. This is the end of us anyway. You're going to kill us the moment you find the treasure. *If* you find the treasure."

I held my breath. Dad was really taking a risk, but I was proud of him for standing up to those goons. If they weren't going to let us go, at least he didn't have to give them the treasure.

"We'll look around ourselves," Hawk said. "Tie them up, Chester. How far can it be from here to the treasure? A few feet? We'll dig up the whole cave if we have to."

He hung the lantern on a hook of coral sticking out of the ceiling. Then he and Chester began frantically searching all of the walls. They sloshed over every inch of the floor, hunting for a secret passage way or a lever or a trap door or another message. But they didn't find anything.

Time seemed to stand still as Dad, Lisa, and I stood silently against one wall and felt the water rise. It crept up inch by inch as the hours went by, swirling the macabre

107

collection of bones with it. Our grisly fate would be the same as those who had come here before us—the English missionary, the French explorer, the Russian scientist, and who knows how many others. I shivered as I realized that it could be their bones that floated nearer and nearer our faces.

Hawk and Chester swore in frustration. They glared at us.

"What's going on down there, you idiots?" Blackie called.

"One last chance to save yourself," Hawk screamed at Dad, grabbing a bone and shaking it in Dad's face.

"I don't know any more than you do at this point, boys," Dad maintained. "I guess you're out of luck."

"Wrong, dead wrong, Captain," Hawk yelled hysterically. "You're the one who's out of luck!"

I stiffened.

"You've been treating us unfairly ever since we came on your crew. You take the biggest share of the loot. You grab all the glory!" he spat angrily. "You treat us like dogs and think we should be overjoyed to lick your boots! But no more!"

He had really gone crazy. Dad didn't treat his crew like that. But I could tell by the insane look in Hawk's eyes that it wouldn't be any use to argue with him. His mind had snapped and all he could think about was finding the treasure—or taking a hideous revenge on the person he thought was keeping him from reaching it. The Buzzard's curse had claimed Hawk as another victim, and now he was convinced we were standing in his way!

Hawk thrashed around in the water, cursing and screaming at Dad about how unfair Dad had been and how awful life aboard the ship had been.

Chester egged him on. "That's right, Captain," he added spitefully. "How much gold have you hidden from us? Our shares were so paltry, so puny. We know you're holding out on us."

"That's a lie!" Dad said. "I've always paid everyone fairly."

"You're the one who's a liar!" Hawk shouted. Suddenly, he lunged toward us, his eyes glowing red in the light of the lantern. He grabbed a bone and smashed Dad across the side of the head with it.

Things seemed to move in slow motion for me. Dad toppled over into the water. Hawk and Chester watched, surprised, then bolted for the rope.

Somehow Lisa worked her hands free and managed to pull Dad's head above water just as Blackie pulled the crooks from the cave with the rope.

"You can't leave us down here," she cried.

"We'll be back," Hawk told her, a broad grin splitting his evil face. "At the next low tide."

"Yeah," Chester added. "It's too bad you won't be around to help us find the treasure. This chamber will be flooded in an hour and you'll all be dead!"

Their laughter rang out overhead as they climbed out of the hole and pulled the rope up after them.

"Don't worry, Lisa," I said as I tried to stop my heart from pounding out of my chest. "We'll tread water until we reach the top, then climb out the hole, too."

"Good idea," she answered, "and we can . . . "

But just then we heard a rumble from up above. Water poured into the cave through the hole. The tide was coming in. Pretty soon the cave would be full of water. We were trapped!

I looked around the death chamber in the fading light. I had a nightmarish vision of my own bones mixing with all these hundreds of bones of people from ages past who'd met the same unspeakable fate that was now going to be ours.

CHAPTER 11
The Secret Of The Buzzard's Lair

I tried to shake from my mind the hideous vision of my bones mingled with the other bones. "How's Dad?" I asked Lisa. The water was now up to my waist. My hands were still tied behind my back.

"Out cold, and he's bleeding," Lisa said. She used a little water to wipe the side of his face where blood oozed from a long gash.

"Help me out of my ropes," I said. "How did you get loose so fast, anyway?"

She showed me a small knife. "I stole it while I was cooking yesterday. As Bob would say, fail to plan . . . "

"Plan to fail," I finished.

"Hold Dad up," she instructed.

I pressed Dad against the wall with my knees and chest while Lisa sawed at my wet ropes. "Hurry," I said, "the water's getting higher every minute."

"I'm trying, Brian," she said. Finally I felt

the rope give way. "There!"

I rubbed my wrists and grabbed Dad under his arms. "Dad! Dad! Wake up. We've got to find a way out of here." Then I used Lisa's knife to cut the rope that bound Dad's hands.

Dad groaned. He opened his eyes. "To the sea," he mumbled. "A passage to the sea." Then his eyes rolled back and he passed out again.

"What does that mean?" I shouted. The water level rose as the waves washed over the beach above us. But each time the wave went back out to sea, the water level in our death chamber was a little higher. I struggled to keep Dad's head above water. But a voice inside me kept asking, *Why bother? No one has ever escaped from this watery grave. You'll be the next victims.*

"I want to go home," Lisa said.

"Me, too," I told her. I put my free arm around her and gave her a hug. "I love you, Lisa. You're the best sister a guy could ever have."

"I love you, too, Brian. I don't want to die like this."

"Neither do I. That's why we've got to think. What did the Buzzard mean by *passage to the sea*. There has to be a way out of here, maybe in the direction of the sea."

The water was up to our necks now. With

each ebb and flow of the tide we had to jump and lift Dad above the rising swell. Bones floated all around us, making eerie clicking noises as they bumped into each other. Again my nightmare vision crowded all other thoughts from my mind.

As we searched desperately for a way out of the Buzzard's death chamber, the tide was slowly rising. Soon it was so high that we started treading water. I held Dad up and Lisa tried to keep the flashlight above the water.

I knew our time was running out. I thought about Mom and the ship. I thought about what the rest of my life would have been like, all the people I would have met and the things I would have done. I knew then I would never do them.

Then I started to get angry instead of feeling sorry for myself. Would we be just like all of those other treasure hunters who disappeared without a trace? This was the Buzzard's curse all right, only it was happening to the wrong people. Chester, Blackie, and Hawk were the bad guys. Why weren't they about to suffer our fate?

"Brian," Lisa said, pointing to the far wall, the one closest to the sea. "Watch the water when it rises the next time and check out that corner of the chamber."

Lisa took Dad from my grasp and gave me the flashlight. Then sputtering and kicking against the pull of the tide, I swam over nearer the corner and watched. The water came in, bubbling through a narrow crack in the chamber wall. Bones clogged the crack and I pulled them away. When the water went out the next time, it retreated quickly. That meant there had to be a narrow passageway somewhere back there.

I stuck my arm as far into the crack as I could and shined the light. At the end I could just make out some kind of metal plate.

"I think there's a door or something down there," I said.

"Can we get through?" Lisa asked.

"I don't know," I told her, "but it's our only hope. Can you hold Dad while I get some of these bones out of the way?"

"I can do anything if it means getting us out of here."

"That's the spirit," I said, plunging my arm into the crack.

Centuries of debris and broken bones clogged the passageway. That must have been why Chester and Hawk had missed it earlier. Little by little I threw the rubble back out into the main chamber. Soon the water was so high I had to dive into the passageway, grab as many bones as I could,

114

and then back out into the chamber.

"There's no more time," Lisa gasped I emerged with the last of the junk. Her h... was touching the ceiling of the chamber and it was all she could do to hold Dad up. I had to tip my head to the side to take a breath.

"When the water lowers this time," I panted, "I'll go in and hope that door opens at the end."

"Okay," she said, her eyes holding mine. "I'll watch over Dad."

I felt the water recede ever so slightly, then whoosh out, opening the passageway for a split second.

I plunged into the dark passageway. I reached the door and yanked my hardest, but it didn't budge.

Beyond the walls of the passageway I could hear the roar of the incoming wave. This was it. Our last chance. When this wave rushed into the passageway, it would fill the whole space, leaving no air for us to breathe.

I took a breath and dove underwater. I felt all around the door with my fingertips, my lungs starting to burn. At first I felt nothing, only smooth metal. Then my thumb touched something that felt like a lever and I pushed down with all of my might.

I heard a latch click underwater and then the door swung open into the passageway.

With a rush of water I pushed myself through. Lisa followed, dragging Dad.

To my dismay, there was water in the opening beyond. Then I stood up and filled my aching lungs with the dry, musty air. It was the sweetest breath I had ever taken. Lisa yanked Dad's head out of the water.

Behind us, the ancient door creaked shut as the waves pulled it. Though I felt for a lever on the inside, it was completely smooth.

"From one grave to another," I murmured.

"At least this one has air," Lisa said. She shined the flashlight into the space beyond us.

We gasped in utter disbelief. Cutlasses adorned the walls. Golden plates and crystal goblets sat on jeweled tables. A spy glass was propped on a tripod in the exact position that the Buzzard must have left it 300 years ago.

We were in the Buzzard's lair! And maybe our own burial chamber.

The light flickered as we stepped out of the entrance pool and onto the dry chamber floor. The room was musty with the smell of centuries-old air. But at least it was dry and I dragged Dad to a flat spot.

He groaned and spit up water.

"Dad?" I said. "Dad, wake up!"

The flashlight flickered again and almost went out.

"I think the batteries got wet," Lisa said.

"Maybe there's something around here," I said, glancing around. My eyes fell on an ancient torch, preserved perfectly in the room. There were flint and steel beside it.

I struck them together and made a spark. Immediately the torch caught fire and filled the treasure chamber with light.

Dad opened his eyes and looked around, holding his head and rising on one elbow. "You've found it! You've found the Buzzard's lair!"

"We're still trapped," I told him.

"But at least we're safe for the moment. What happened after Hawk hit me?" he asked.

We told him about Hawk and Chester leaving us for dead in the outer chamber and about how scared we were when the water kept rising.

"Then Lisa spotted a crack and I dug the bones out," I said.

"And Brian swam into the passageway, opened the door, and here we are," Lisa said.

"And you did all this, dragging your unconscious father," Dad said. "You two are the best partners this treasure hunter ever had."

"Look at this stuff," I exclaimed. "Look at these statues, these clothes. The clothes are

117

perfect, not rotted at all. Every jewel is still shiny and there isn't even any dust or cobwebs."

"That's because this chamber is airtight," Dad said, looking around. "I'm sure the Buzzard planned this. Even if someone did find his treasure, they would never get away with it, because they would be sealed in his lair forever."

"There has to be a way out," I said. "Maybe we can break down the door at low tide and go back the way we came."

"I think we'd end up buried alive," Dad said, gesturing toward the pool. "Look at all the timbers and mechanisms attached to the door. They're there to destroy the room if anyone tampers with it or tries to get out once they're inside. Besides, there's not enough oxygen in this chamber to last until the next low tide."

Together we looked around in the room, examining the treasure: ship logs, boots, a jeweled belt buckle, a small golden statue of a saint, clothing, and old weapons and instruments. It was beyond belief, all the stuff in the chamber. Then finally I spotted what we had really been looking for. Set back in a notch in the wall was an ornate wooden chest with what looked like silver hardware.

We all stared at the chest speechless. Even

though we knew we would never escape to show it to the rest of the world, we gazed in awe at the Buzzard's treasure chest.

"Open it, Dad," I said.

Dad grabbed a cutlass from the wall and pried open the lid to the chest. With a creak and a groan, the lid of the 300-year-old chest slowly opened. We gasped as the light from the flaming torch glinted off the gold coins. The chest was full of gold. But then I remembered bitterly that we could never use it. Our bones would become the treasure's guardians.

Dad reached in to scoop out the coins. But he cried out suddenly. He emptied his hands. Down fell a few gold coins. But a handful of wood shavings also fluttered down.

"What the . . . " he cried. "It's only one layer of gold." He searched beneath the coins, but found only more wood shavings.

Then, with another cry, he lifted up a stone tablet with some words carved in French. Lisa and I jumped to his side.

"Where's the rest of the treasure?" I asked. "Hidden somewhere else in the room?"

"I don't think so, Brian" Dad said. "Listen to this. I'll translate it for you." He read the Buzzard's message aloud.

"To the fool who has wasted his days in search of my treasure, I commend you. You have understood my code, but not my message. I dumped the rest of my gold into the sea. Enjoy the gold in this chest, for it is all you will ever see of the Buzzard's riches."

I could almost hear the echo of the pirate's evil laugh. It wasn't enough that we were to die searching for his treasure. Now we knew the bitter, bitter truth. There was no treasure. The Buzzard was having the last hideous laugh on us. He really was crazy for not even keeping the money for himself.

Dad slumped back against the wall and stared at the stone tablet. We sat down next to him and were silent. Now the desperate situation we were in hit home, and we clung to each other for our last moments.

After what seemed like a long time, Dad was the first to speak. In a quiet voice filled with emotion, he said, "You know, I don't even care about the treasure anymore. These past few days have taught me a lot about what's really important to me. You kids and your mom have taken a back seat to my treasure hunting for years."

His voice quivered with emotion and he tried to continue. "I-I know I haven't always been the best father. It seems like I was always promising to make time for the family and never did. I'm sorry I didn't find the time to be with you guys more."

"That's not true, Dad," Lisa said. "We've been with you all the time, hunting for treasure, living on the ship."

"You were with me, but I didn't pay enough attention to you," he continued. "I let my job get in the way of what really matters—my family."

"You matter to us, too, Dad," I told him.

"And look what happened," Dad said. "I've had enough adventure. If we get out of here, I'm going to quit treasure hunting and spend the rest of my time getting to know my family—like I should have in the first place."

Dad reached out and hugged us close to him. "I love you guys," he said, "and I'm sorry for everything."

"We love you, Dad," I said.

We got quiet again, listening to the sound of our own breathing and the sound of the waves crashing somewhere up above us. Something popped into my head. "What do you think the Buzzard meant by 'you have understood my code, but not my message'?" I asked Dad.

"Maybe he meant that the true treasure is life itself," Dad replied thoughtfully. "And if we do get out of here, things are going to be different. I promise."

Lisa, who had been quiet for a while, said suddenly, "There *has* to be a way out of here."

She stood up and walked over to the treasure chest. "I can't believe the Buzzard meant for whoever found this to die here."

She started taking the wood chips out of the chest.

"There are no more coins," I said.

"I know that. But maybe there's a clue of some kind in here. The Buzzard loved clues," she said. "What was the last symbol on your chart, Dad?"

"A triangle," Dad said. "I never figured it out."

"What about the skeleton picture with the triangle on his head in the cave?" I asked.

"It must have something to do with the last clue," Dad answered. "But I understand the last line of the code though. 'To the sea, riches, true treasure, fullest pleasure.'"

"I understand it, too. He dumped his riches into the sea to prove that he could outsmart anyone, even the person who finally figured out his code," I said. "But what about the triangle. Could it be another mountain?"

"Oh!" Lisa gasped. "There's something down here." She reached down into the bottom of the chest and pulled up a false wooden bottom. Lying beneath it was a black velvet pouch.

"Open it up," I said. "Quick!"

She pulled the drawstring open and

dropped a strange triangular-shaped stone into the palm of her hand. "It says something," she said, handing it to Dad.

Dad looked at the carvings and looked back up at us.

"What does it say?" I asked.

Dad shook his head. "It says something like, 'I am the key out of the grave.'"

A last hope! We all knew we only had a short time to figure out how this stone could lead us out of the death chamber. The air was already getting stuffy and it was becoming harder and harder to breathe.

We searched the walls, the floor, the ceiling. We examined every corner, studied every drawing and carving, and looked under every single thing in the chamber. Finally, in an alcove at the end of the chamber, far away from the passageway we entered by, Lisa found it. There was a triangular depression in the coral wall. Around it, we could just make out the outline of a skull, carved into the wall.

Lisa cried out and we were at her side in an instant. "Should I push it in?" Lisa asked.

"What have we got to lose?" Dad answered. He gave each of us a hug and nodded for Lisa to put the stone into the matching slot. Lisa carefully fitted the stone into the slot in the wall. She looked at us. Then she pressed the stone in as far as it would go, like a key in some mystical door. We heard a faint sound like a click.

Then we stepped back into the chamber.

At first nothing happened. We looked at each other, disappointment mirrored in our eyes.

But then the walls started shaking. The ceiling shook. Sand fell from the ceiling, choking the chamber with dust. I couldn't breath, I couldn't see. We were being buried alive!

We heard a roar and I braced myself for the end. I reached for Dad and Lisa.

A wall of sand poured into one end of the alcove, followed by a rush of fresh air. As if by magic, the walls crumbled away and revealed a set of carved handles on a rock wall. We sprang forward. Dad pushed Lisa and me up the rock steps. Then he followed us up as rock, sand, and sea water rushed into the chamber behind us.

The sun was just rising as we emerged onto the beach. I had never expected to see it again. Suddenly, I heard another sound over the roar of the collapsing chamber and the pounding surf of the ocean. Looking into the sky, I saw two helicopters. And scanning the beach, I saw a large group of island police, some running our way, others riding in trucks.

The trucks reached us just as the helicopters touched down on the beach about a hundred feet from us. Mom jumped from one helicopter. She had a huge smile on her face and tears in her eyes.

"Stephen!" Mom shouted, rushing toward us. "Brian! Lisa! I can't believe it. You're all right!"

We hugged and kissed about a million times. We were all crying, but I didn't care. This was the best moment of my life.

When I looked up, I saw Bob and Melanie standing near, with a group of police. They had made it through to the police after all!

"What about Chester and Hawk and Blackie?" Dad asked.

"We caught them as they were trying to leave with your ship," the chief of police explained. "We had the ship under surveillance ever since it returned, since we knew it was the only way they could leave the island. They told us where you were, but we were afraid you were dead. They explained the whole thing, how they waited at the camp for you, how Chester tried to fool the Attwaters into thinking he was an island police officer . . . they confessed the whole plot. We're just lucky we found you in time."

"My parents are all right too," Melanie said. "The police found them tied up in a storage shed behind our house."

Bob came forward with a black-haired woman in a police uniform. Before she told us, I knew it was Officer Chris Martin.

"Blackie read my name in the newspaper when I received a citation for ten years of service," she explained with a laugh. "He made the mistake of assuming only men are named Chris."

"We found the Buzzard's lair, Mom," I said.

"The treasure?" Bob asked.

"Sort of," I said.

"It's not the same treasure we were looking for," Dad said, pulling Mom, Lisa, and me close. "The Buzzard's fifty million dollar treasure is lost forever. But that wily old Buzzard gave us our lives and a few trinkets to show to the world. Most of all, he taught me a lesson I promise never to forget."

"I don't understand," Mom said. "What did he teach you?"

"That my greatest treasure has nothing to do with gold and jewels. My fortune is my family. And if I ever forget it again, you kids knock me over the head with a bone or something."

I grinned. "I just happen to know where I can find a lot of those."

About the Author

Cindy Savage wrote *The Buzzard's Treasure* after reading about the Seychelles islands and the legend of the lost treasure in an unsolved mysteries book.

Much of the information in this book is based on a real legend. For instance, the Buzzard really was a French pirate named Olivier le Vasseur who hid treasure somewhere on the Seychelles island of Mahé.

The legend also states that the Buzzard threw a scroll containing clues into the crowd just before he was hanged for piracy. Many of the clues Cindy used in this book are the same ones the Buzzard wrote on that scroll.

Cindy lives in a big rambling house on a tiny farm in northern California with her husband, Greg, and her six children: Linda, Laura, Brian, Kevin, Warren, and Lisa. In fact, she named the main characters in this book after two of her children.

Some of her other books for Willowisp Press are *The Curse of Blood Swamp*, *The Zoo Crew,* and the *Forever Friends* series.